AGATHA RAISIN AND THE WIZARD OF EVESHAM

M.C. Beaton

CHIVERS

British Library Cataloguing in Publication Data available

This Large Print edition published by BBC Audiobooks Ltd, Bath, 2008.
Published by arrangement with Constable & Robinson Ltd.

U.K. Hardcover ISBN 978 1 405 64512 6
U.K. Softcover ISBN 978 1 405 64513 3

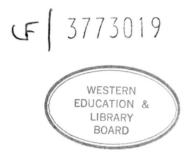
Printed and bound in Great Britain by
CPI Antony Rowe, Chippenham, Wiltshire

*The author wishes to thank
Marie Steele of Thomas Oliver,
the real wizard of Evesham,
for her help in this book.*

Chapter One

The weather was tropical. And this was England and this was Evesham in the Cotswolds. Agatha Raisin drove into the car park at Merstow Green, turned off the air-conditioning, switched off the engine and braced herself to meet the wall of soupy heat which she knew would greet her the minute she stepped out of the car.

Like many, she had decided that all the scares about the greenhouse effect were simply lies made up by eco-terrorists. But this August had seen clammy, sweaty days followed by monsoon thunderstorms at night. Most odd.

Agatha groaned as she left her car and walked across to the parking-ticket machine. What a hell of a day to decide to get one's hair tinted!

She returned to her car and pasted the ticket on the window and then bent down and squinted at herself in the driving-mirror. Her hair was still dark brown but now streaked with purple.

Agatha had gone into a mild depression following her 'last case'. Mrs Agatha Raisin fancied herself to be a detective to rival the fictional ones like Poirot and Lord Peter Wimsey. She was a stocky middle-aged woman with good legs, a round face and small bearlike eyes which looked suspiciously out at the world. Her hair had always been her pride, thick and brown and glossy.

But only that week she had discovered grey hairs, nasty grey hairs appearing all over. She had bought one of those colour rinses but it had turned the grey purple. 'Go to Mr John,' advised Mrs Bloxby, the vicar's wife. 'His place is in the High Street in Evesham. He's supposed to be very good. They say he's a wizard at tinting hair.'

So Agatha had made the appointment and here she was in Evesham, a town situated some ten miles from her home village of Carsely.

The cynics say Evesham is famous for dole and asparagus. Situated beside the river Avon in the Vale of Evesham, the Garden of England, well-known for its nurseries, orchards and, of course, asparagus, Evesham nonetheless can present itself to the visitor who comes to see its historical buildings as a down-at-heel town. Despite the increasing population, shops keep closing up and the boards over the windows are decorated with old Evesham scenes by local artists, so that sometimes it seems a town of pictures and thrift shops. Enormous fecund women trundle push-chairs with small children. The fashion they favour is leggings topped by a baggy blouse. As columnist and TV celebrity Anne

Robinson said, she thought leggings came along with push-chairs and babies.

Agatha sometimes thought that a lot of the clothes shops closed down because the buyers would not look out of the window at the size of the female population and stocked only up to size sixteen instead of up to size twenty-two.

She walked over to the High Street, not even stopping to look at the magnificent bulk of the old churches. Agatha was not interested in history as James Lacey, the love of her life, her neighbour, was off once more on his travels, leaving his cottage deserted and Agatha depressed and with grey hairs on her head.

The hairdresser's was simply called Mr John. Mrs Bloxby had urged Agatha to make sure she got Mr John in person.

And there it was, glittering in the heat of the High Street, a discreet shop frontage with MR JOHN emblazoned in curly brass letters over the door.

Agatha pushed open the door and went in. No air-conditioning, of course. This was Britain and there were too many recent memories of cold summers for shopkeepers to decide to put in air-conditioning.

A receptionist marked off Agatha's name in the book and called to a thin, pimply girl to escort Agatha to the salon. Agatha began to wish she had not come. She trudged through to a room at the back and the girl said she would fetch Mr John.

Agatha gazed sullenly at her reflection in the mirror. She felt old and frumpy.

Then suddenly behind her in the mirror, a vision appeared and a pleasant voice said, 'Good afternoon, Mrs Raisin. I'm Mr John.'

Agatha blinked. Mr John was tall and very, very handsome. He had thick blond hair and very bright blue eyes, startlingly blue, as blue as a kingfisher's wing. His face was lightly tanned.

'Now what have we here?' he said.

'We have purple hair,' snapped Agatha, feeling diminished in front of this handsome vision.

'It's easily remedied. Would you also like me to style your hair?'

Agatha, who usually kept her hair short, had let it grow quite long. She shrugged. In for a penny, in for a pound. 'Why not?'

'You're not local, are you?' Mr John stirred the hair tint with strong, well-manicured hands.

'No, I'm from London.' Agatha had no intention of telling Mr John or anyone about her childhood background in a Birmingham slum. 'I had my own public relations business and sold up and took early retirement and moved to Carsely.'

'Pretty village.'

'Yes, very pleasant.'

4

'And does your husband like it?'

'My husband is dead.'

His hands hovered above her head. 'Raisin. Raisin? That name rings a bell.'

'It should do. He was murdered.'

'Ah, yes, I remember. How terrible for you.'

'I'm over it now. I hadn't seen him in years anyway.'

'Well, an attractive lady like yourself won't remain single for long.'

'I am sure you mean well and that's what you say to all your dreary customers,' said Agatha tetchily, 'but I am well aware of what I look like.'

'Ah, but I haven't done your hair before. By the time I've finished with you, you'll be fighting them off with clubs.'

Agatha suddenly laughed. 'You're very sure of your skill.'

'I have every reason to be.'

'So if you're that good, why Evesham?'

'Why not? I like Evesham. The people are nice. I am king here. I might be lost among the competition in London. There you are. Now, I'll set the timer. Sharon, a coffee and some magazines for Mrs Raisin.'

A woman had entered and was sitting in the chair alongside Agatha. 'Ready to have your colour done again, Maggie?' Mr John greeted her.

'If you think so,' said Maggie, gazing up at him with adoring eyes.

5

'Did your husband like the new style?'

'He doesn't like anything about me.' Maggie's voice had taken on a querulous moan. 'Insults from morning to night. I tell you, John, if it weren't for you bucking me up, I'd kill myself.'

'There, now. You'll feel better when I've finished with you.'

As Agatha waited for the tint to take effect and more customers were dealt with, some by a couple of assistants, Agatha was amazed at the personal revelations that were poured into the hairdressers' ears.

She covertly watched Mr John as he moved about, admiring his athletic body and his blond hair, and oh, those blue, blue eyes.

Agatha began to feel alive for the first time in weeks.

The timer rang and she was escorted through to a hand-basin and the tint was washed out. Then back to Mr John, who began to put her hair up in rollers.

'I thought it would be a blow-dry.'

'I'm going to put your hair up . . . Agatha. It is Agatha, isn't it?'

A less glorious-looking hairdresser would have been told sharply that it was Mrs Raisin. Agatha nodded.

'You'll love it.'

'I've never had my hair up before. I've always had it short.'

He clicked his tongue. 'Ladies who don't

6

think as much of themselves as they should, always get their hair cut short. Show me a woman with her hair cut to the bone and I'll show you an example of really low self-worth. Tell you what, if you don't like it, I'll take it down again and cut it.'

Agatha reluctantly gave her approval although she could feel sweat trickling down her body. How did Mr John keep so cool?

She was just beginning to feel she had been under the hot drier for hours when she was rescued and taken back to Mr John.

As he worked busily away, Agatha looked in delight as her new appearance emerged. Her hair was glossy and brown once more, but swept up in a French pleat and then arranged around her square face in a way that made it looked thinner. She forgot about the heat. She smiled up at Mr John in sheer gratitude.

It was only when she was walking back down the High Street, squinting in shop windows to admire her reflection, that she realized she had not made another appointment. But Agatha had mostly done her own hair, getting it cut in London on her occasional visits.

Once home, she opened all the doors and windows to try to let in some fresh air. Her two cats darted out into the garden and then promptly lay down on the grass, lethargic in the sun.

She looked at her silent phone. To add to

her depression, it never seemed to ring. Her friend, Detective Sergeant Bill Wong was on holiday; Sir Charles Fraith, with whom she had been involved on a couple of cases, was abroad somewhere; James Lacey was God only knew where; and even Roy Silver, her former employee, had not troubled to ring.

Then she remembered there was to be a meeting of the Carsely Ladies' Society that evening. A good opportunity to show off her new hair-style.

Mrs Bloxby was hosting the society at the vicarage and because of the heat had set out chairs and tables in the vicarage garden.

Agatha's hair-style was much admired. 'Where did you go?' asked Mrs Friendly, a plump, cheerful woman who usually lived up to her name. She was a relative newcomer to the village and hailed as an antidote to that other relative newcomer, Mrs Darry, who was nibbling a piece of cake with rabbitlike concentration.

'Mr John in Evesham,' said Agatha.

To her surprise, Mrs Friendly's face creased up like that of a hurt baby. 'I wouldn't go there,' she said, lowering her voice to a whisper.

'Why?' Agatha stared rudely at Mrs Friendly's hair, which was a mousy brown and hanging in damp wisps round her hot face.

'Nothing,' muttered Mrs Friendly. 'One

8

hears stories.'

'About Mr John?'

'Yes.'

'What stories?'

'Must talk to Mrs Bloxby.' Mrs Friendly moved away. Agatha stared after her and then shrugged. She was joined by Miss Simms, Carsely's unmarried mother and secretary of the society. 'You look drop-dead gorgeous, Mrs Raisin.' Agatha had long ago given up asking other members to call her by her first name. They all seemed to enjoy the old-fashioned formality of second names. Miss Simms was wearing a brief pair of shorts with a halter-top and her usual spiked heels. 'Where did you go?'

'Mr John in Evesham.'

'Oh, I went there once to get my hair done. I was bridesmaid at my sister Glad's wedding. He did it ever so pretty, but I didn't like him.'

'Why?'

'Awful patronizing, he was. Gushed around the richer customers.'

Agatha shrugged. 'It doesn't really matter what a hairdresser's like, does it?'

'To me it does. I mean to say, I don't like anyone I don't like touching me.'

The meeting was called to order. They were to give one of their concerts over at Ancombe. Agatha's heart sank. Ladies' Society concerts were truly awful, long evenings of shrill

9

singing and bad sketches.

Mrs Darry piped up, her eyes gleaming in her ferrety face. She was wearing a tweed skirt, blouse and tweed jacket but seemed unaffected by the heat. 'Why doesn't Mrs Raisin ever volunteer to do anything?'

'Why don't you?' snapped Agatha.

'Because *I* am doing the teas.'

'I have no talent,' said Agatha.

Mrs Darry gave a shrill laugh. 'Neither do any of the others, but that doesn't stop them.'

'Really,' protested Mrs Bloxby, 'that was unkind.'

Miss Simms, who had volunteered to do her impersonation of Cher, glared. 'Jealous cow,' she said.

'I've a good mind to let you do the teas yourselves,' said Mrs Darry.

There was a silence. Then Agatha said, 'I'll do it.'

'Good idea,' said Miss Simms.

Mrs Darry got to her feet. 'Then if you don't need my services, I'm going home.'

She stalked out of the garden.

Agatha bit her lip. She didn't want to be bothered catering for a bunch of women in all this heat.

The depression which had lifted because of her visit to the hairdresser came down around her again like a black cloud. This is your life, Agatha Raisin. Trapped in a Cotswold village, cut off from excitement, cut off from adventure, doing teas for a bunch of boring women.

She trudged home afterwards. There did not seem to be a breath of air.

She opened all the windows. She looked at the silent phone. Could anyone have rung when she was out? She dialled 1571 for the Call Minder. 'You have *one* message,' said the carefully elocuted voice of the computer. 'Would you like to hear it?'

'Of course I would, you silly bitch,' growled Agatha.

There was a silence and then the voice said primly, 'I did not hear that. Would you like to hear your message?'

There was a click and then the well-modulated tones of Sir Charles Fraith sounded down the line, 'Hello, Aggie. Fancy dinner tomorrow?'

Agatha brightened. Although she had been wary of Charles because of a one-night stand when they had both been in Cyprus, a night of sex which had seemed to mean very little to him, the thought of going out to dinner and showing off her new hair-style appealed greatly.

She dialled his number and got his Call Minder and left a message asking him to call for her at eight o'clock the following evening.

Her depression once more lifted, she went upstairs and had a bath and went to bed. She had left her hair pinned up, but as she lay on her hot pillow the pins bored into her head. At last she rose and took all the pins out and went back to bed, tossing and turning all night in the suffocating heat. Thunder rolled and the rain came down about two in the morning but did nothing to freshen the air.

When she rose in the morning, it was to find her hair was a disaster, damp with heat, and dishevelled with all the tossing about.

As soon as she knew the salon would be open, she phoned Mr John's receptionist to see if she could have an appointment for that day. 'I am so sorry, Mrs Raisin,' said the receptionist on a rather smug note. 'Mr John is fully booked.'

'Put him on.'

'I beg your parding?'

'I said let me talk to him . . . now!'

'Oh, very well.'

'Agatha!' Mr John welcomed her like an old friend.

'I've got a dinner date and my hair is a wreck. Could you possibly fit me in?'

'I would like to help you out. Let me see. Give me the book, Josie.'

There was a rustling of pages and then he came back on the phone. 'You had your hair washed yesterday, so what I could do is just put it in rollers and then pin it up, but it would need to be five o'clock.'

Agatha thought quickly. She would have plenty of time to get her hair done, get back home and washed and changed in time for Charles. 'Lovely,' she said. 'I'll be there.'

She then went up to the bedroom and swung open the doors of the wardrobe. What to wear? There was that little black dress she hadn't worn since Cyprus. He had liked it. She tried it on. It hung loose on her body. How odd, thought Agatha, that depression could do so effectively what all those diets and exercise had not. She had lost weight.

She decided to drive into Mircester and look for something new.

The steering-wheel of her car scorched her hands and she was up out of the village and speeding along the Fosse before the air-conditioning worked.

Mircester shimmered under ferocious heat. She was able to find a parking place without difficulty. A lot of people seemed to have decided to stay at home. Agatha put on her sunglasses and squinted up at the sky. Not a cloud in sight. She made her way to Harris Street off the main square, which boasted a line of expensive boutiques.

She went in and out of one hot shop after another until she felt she could not bear to try on another dress. Perhaps it would be better to settle for one of her old dresses. It might be a bit loose but that would be all to the good, for any restaurant they went to would not have air-conditioning.

Agatha had just decided to forget about the

whole thing when, looking along an alley which led off Harris Street and down to the abbey, she noticed the weekly market was in full swing. She would buy some fresh vegetables for salad. Once she was in the market and heading for the vegetable stalls, she noticed several stalls full of brightly coloured clothes. In one of them, a dress caught her eye. It was of fine scarlet cotton with a design of white lotus flowers. It had a cool, flowing line. Agatha fingered it. An Indian trader appeared at her elbow. 'Nice dress,' he said.

Agatha hesitated and then asked, 'How much?'

'Fourteen pounds.'

Again Agatha hesitated. It was very cheap. It might wrinkle or even fall apart. She had been prepared to spend a couple of hundred pounds. 'Tell you what,' said the trader wearily, 'you can have it for twelve.'

'Okay, I'll take it.'

He stuffed the dress in an old plastic bag.

'Hot, isn't it?' Agatha handed over the money.

'And don't tell me I ought to be used to it,' he said gloomily. 'I was born in Birmingham.'

Agatha was about to say, 'So was I,' but then left the words unsaid. She was ashamed of her background.

She tried on the dress as soon as she got home. It was very attractive and, once she had

14

added a thick gold necklace, looked quite expensive.

Now for Mr John.

Evesham seemed even hotter than Mircester. Agatha suddenly wished she had her old, simple hair-style which she could wash and arrange herself.

But there was Mr John, cool and handsome as ever. 'Got a date?' he asked.

'Yes.'

'Anyone special?'

Agatha could not resist bragging.

'Actually, he's a baronet.'

'Very grand. Which baronet?'

'Sir Charles Fraith.'

'And how did you come to meet him?'

Agatha was about to say, 'On a case,' but she did not like the implication that such as Agatha Raisin could not know anyone with a title, so she said airily, 'He's in my set.'

And hope that shuts you up, she thought.

'Pity,' he said.

'What's a pity?'

'You'll think this very forward of me, but I was thinking of asking you out myself.'

'Why?' asked Agatha in surprise.

'You're a very attractive woman.'

And a rich one, thought Agatha cynically. But then Mr John was so very handsome with his intense blue eyes and blond hair. If James came back and if James saw them going out together, perhaps he would be jealous;

15

perhaps he would be prompted into saying huskily, 'I always loved you, Agatha.'

'Sorry.' Mr John dug a pin into the back of Agatha's hair and her rosy dream burst like a brightly coloured soap bubble.

'Perhaps some evening,' said Agatha cautiously. 'Let me think about it.'

But his invitation gave her a warm little glow, and he was a wizard at fashioning her hair into that elegant style.

Agatha made her way out to her car which she had parked on a double yellow line. 'Look where that car's parked!' hissed a woman at her ear.

Agatha swung round. A dumpy, frumpy woman with thick glasses was glaring at her. Agatha shrugged, walked to her car and opened the door.

'It's yours!' gasped the woman. 'Don't you know it's illegal to park there?'

Agatha turned and faced her. 'I am not obstructing the traffic or getting in anyone's way,' she said evenly. 'Nor am I responsible for the mad parking arrangements of Evesham or for the stupid one-way system. But I wonder where someone like you gets off on this hot day abusing motorists. Go home, have a cup of tea, put your feet up. Get a life!'

And deaf to the insults that began to pour about her ears, Agatha got in and drove off.

*   *   *

16

Charles arrived promptly at eight o'clock. He gave her a chaste kiss on the cheek. 'Like the hair, Aggie. And the dress. In fact, I bought a dress like that in the market in Mircester this afternoon for my aunt. She was grumbling about not having anything cool to wear.'

'I bought this one in Harrods,' lied Agatha. 'The one in the market must have been a cheap copy.' But her pleasure in her appearance had diminished. 'Where are we eating?'

'I thought we would go to the Little Chef.'

'I am not being taken out to a Little Chef. You *are* cheap, Charles.'

'I like the food,' he said defensively. 'I suppose you want foreign muck. Well, give me a whisky while I think of something.'

Agatha poured him a whisky and he settled in a chair cradling his glass between small, well-manicured hands. He was a slight, fair-haired man. Agatha had never known his age. He had mild, sensitive features and she had originally thought he might be only in his late thirties. But she had later decided he was probably in his mid-forties. He was wearing a shirt open at the neck and had slung his jacket over a chair.

'I know,' he said. 'The Jolly Roger at Ancombe, that new pub.'

'I haven't been there and I don't like the sound of it.'

'Friend of mine went the other week. Said the food was good. Besides, they've got a garden with tables. By the way, I saw that detective friend of yours in Mircester; what's his name, Chinese chap?'

'Bill Wong. But he's on holiday!'

'I suppose he's taking it at home. Had a girl on his arm.'

And he hasn't phoned me, thought Agatha. Bill had been her first friend, the old, tougher Agatha, driven by career and ambition, never having had any time before to make friends. She could feel the old black edges of that depression hovering on the horizon of her mind.

They set out for Ancombe and parked outside the Jolly Roger, formerly called the Green Man. Inside it was everything that shouted poor food to Agatha—fishing nets, murals of pirates, and waiters and barmen dressed in striped tops and knee-breeches with plastic 'silver' buckles. Charles led the way through to the garden, which was at least a fraction cooler than the inside. A roguish waiter who introduced himself as Henry handed them two large, gaudily coloured menus.

'Oh, shit,' grumbled Agatha. 'Listen to this. Captain Hook's scrumptious potato dip. And what about Barbary Coast Chicken with sizzling Long John corn fritters?'

Henry the waiter was hovering. 'Do you

18

remember when they were called hens, and chickens were the fluffy little yellow things?' asked Agatha.

'And now all mutton is lamb, dear,' said Henry with a giggle.

Agatha eyed him with disfavour. 'Just shove off and stop twitching and grinning and we'll call you when we're ready.'

'Well, *really*, I never did.' Henry tossed his head.

'The fact that you haven't lost your virginity is nothing to do with me. Go away.'

'You've hurt his feelings, Aggie,' said Charles equably.

'Don't care,' muttered Agatha. Bill hadn't even bothered to phone her. 'What are you having?'

'I'll have the all-day breakfast. The Dead-Eye Dick Special, and I hope it comes with lots of chips.'

'No starter? Oh well, I'll have a ham salad.'

'They can't have anything described simply as ham salad.'

'It's described as South Sea Roast pig, sliced and on a bed of crunchy salad with Hard Tack croutons.'

'Oh. Wine?'

'Why not?'

Charles signalled to the waiter, ordered their meals and a carafe of house wine.

'No vintage for me?' asked Agatha.

'I wouldn't bother in a place like this.'

'So why did you bring me to a place like this?'

'God, you're sour this evening, Agatha. Am I to assume that James is not around?'

'No, he's away somewhere.'

'And didn't even say goodbye? Yes, I can see by the look on your face.'

'Men are so immature.'

'That's what you women always throw at us.'

'Well, it's true.'

'It's a necessary part of the masculine make-up. It enables us to dream greater dreams and bring them about. Have you ever wondered why all the great inventors are men?'

'Because women never had a chance.'

'Wrong. Women are pragmatic. They have to be to bring up children. I shall illustrate what I mean with a story.' He rested his chin on his hands and gazed dreamily across at her.

'A chap goes to Cambridge University. The girls there terrify him and they're only interested in rugger-buggers anyway and he's the academic type. So he falls in love with a fluffy little barmaid, and gets her pregnant and marries her. He gets a first in physics but he has to support his new family, so he takes a job in an insurance office and there he is, up to his neck in a mortgage and car payments and the wife has twins. A few years pass and he begins to spend every weekend down in the

20

garden shed. Wife begins to whine and complain. "We never see you. Sharon and Tracey are missing their dad. What are you *doing?*" At last he tells her. He's building a time machine. Then the shit hits the fan. Will this pay the bills? she rages at him. The Joneses next door have a new deep freeze. When are they going to get one? And so on. So he locks himself into his shed and hammers away while she screams outside.

'Well, he builds his time machine and becomes a billionaire and runs off with a little bit of fluff in the office who is the only woman who really understands him and has supported him, which of course she has, not knowing one word he's been talking about, but likes the excitement of being involved with a married man. He divorces his wife and marries the office girl and the money goes to her head and she joins the Eurotrash and runs off with a racing driver and they all live unhappily ever after. And the moral of that is, men and women are different and should start to accept the differences.'

Agatha laughed. 'Couldn't he have escaped in his time machine?'

'Of course not. He got billions to destroy it. Can't have people zipping around the centuries and messing up history.'

'I never know if you're a male chauvinist oink or just being funny.'

'I'm never funny. Look at the wrinkles on

my forehead, Aggie. Product of deep thought. So what about you? No nice juicy murders?'

'Nothing at all. I am yesterday's sleuth.'

'I should have thought your experiences in Cyprus would have given you enough death and mayhem for life.'

Cyprus. Where she had passed a night with Charles and James had found out about it and things had never been the same again. Agatha would not admit to herself that her relationship with James had been on the rocks for a long time before that.

Charles watched the shadow fall across her eyes and said gently. 'It wouldn't have worked, you know. James is a twenty-per-cent person.'

'I don't understand you.'

'It's like this. You are an eighty-five-per-cent person and James only gives twenty per cent. It's not a case of won't, it's a case of can't. A lot of men are like that but women will never understand. They go on giving. And they think if they go to bed with the twenty-per-center, and they give that last fifteen per cent, they'll miraculously wake up next to a hundred-per-center. Wrong. If they wake up next to him anyway, it'll be a miracle. Probably find a note on the pillow saying, "Gone home to feed the dog," or something like that.'

Agatha remembered nights with James and mornings when he was always up first, when he never referred to the night before or hugged her or kissed her.

'Maybe I was just the wrong woman,' she conceded.

'Trust me, dearest. Any woman is the wrong woman for James.'

'Perhaps I would have been happy to settle for twenty per cent.'

'Liar. Here's our food.'

To Agatha's surprise, the ham was delicious and the salad fresh and crisp.

'So we're never to go detecting again?' Charles asked, pouring ketchup on his chips.

'I can't go around finding bodies to brighten up my life.'

'No more public relations work?'

'None. All my efforts are going towards providing tea and cakes for the ladies of Ancombe.'

'You'll stir something up, Aggie. No new men on the horizon?'

'One very gorgeous man.'

'Who?'

'My hairdresser.'

'Ah, the one that's responsible for the new elegance.'

'Him.'

'Hairdressers are fickle. I remember . . . Never mind.'

'What about *your* love life, Charles?'

'Nothing at the moment.'

They passed the meal reminiscing about their adventures in Cyprus and then he drove her home.

'Am I going to stay the night?' asked Charles as they stood together on Agatha's doorstep.

'No, Charles, I'm not into casual sex.'

'Who says it would be casual?'

'Charles, you demonstrated in Cyprus that I am nothing more than a temporary amusement to you. Has it ever dawned on you that you might be a twenty-per-center yourself?'

'Ouch! But think on this, Aggie. Any eighty-five-per-center who hangs around with twenty-per-centers is just as afraid of commitment.'

He waved to her and went off to his car.

Agatha let herself in, feeling flat. No messages on the phone for her. And what had Bill Wong been thinking of not to phone her?

The sensible thing would be to phone him, and yet Agatha dreaded the idea of finding out she had lost the affection of her first friend.

Life went on. She had to keep moving. Perhaps she would accept Mr John's invitation after all.

Chapter Two

The heat mounted. Ninety-nine degrees Fahrenheit was recorded at Pershore in Worcester. Incidents of road rage mounted, tar melted on the roads, and Agatha Raisin longed for her old shorter haircut.

She realized that the reason she had not the courage to ask for it to be cut was in case she was accused of having low self-worth. Having come to this conclusion, Agatha decided it was all too ridiculous and made another appointment with Mr John. Back to Evesham, where the women had swapped their leggings for shorts. Acres of white, mottled flesh gleamed in the sunlight.

The hairdresser's was as busy as ever. Mr John had two male assistants, one female, and two juniors. Agatha asked if she could use the toilet. The window at the back of the toilet was open to a little weedy yard.

Then Agatha heard a woman whisper urgently, 'I can't go on. You've got to let me off the hook.'

There was the answering mumble of a man's voice.

'I'll kill you!' shouted the woman, suddenly and violently.

Agatha poked her head out of the window, but she could not make out where the voices had come from.

She went back into the salon, had her hair washed and then braced herself to tell Mr John that she wanted her hair cut short. She found herself wrapped into that anxiety of writing scripts of 'I'll say and then he'll say.' It was the lawn-mower syndrome.

Mr Jones goes out to mow the lawn but finds his lawn-mower has broken down. 'Why don't you ask that nice Mr Smith next door if you can borrow his?' suggests his wife.

'I can't do that,' protests Mr Jones. 'Bit of an imposition.'

'Don't be silly,' says his wife. 'You're being childish. Mr Smith is a very nice man.'

All afternoon Mr Jones frets. He will ask Mr Smith for the loan of his lawn-mower and Mr Smith will say, 'Sorry, old chap, I'm using it myself.' Mr Smith will say, 'I don't like lending out things.' Mr Smith will lie. Mr Smith will look shifty and Mr Smith will say, 'Actually, mine's broken as well.'

At last, nagged by his wife, Mr Jones goes and knocks on Mr Smith's door.

When Mr Smith answers the door, Mr Jones shouts, 'Fuck you and your lawn-mower,' and walks away.

So when Agatha barked at Mr John that she wanted her hair cut, she blushed and felt ridiculous when he said mildly, 'There's no need to shout, Agatha.'

He set about snipping busily. Agatha

glanced about the busy salon. It was done in American in Paris Brothel. Gilt mirrors, curtains with bobbles separating the rooms, Toulouse-Lautrec posters. Mr John wore a white coat like an American dentist. His assistants wore pink smocks.

'I heard a funny thing when I was in the toilet,' Agatha began.

'That sounds like the beginning of a dirty joke.'

'No, really. I heard a woman say something like, "I can't go on. You've got to let me off the hook." She was answered by some man. Then she said, "I'll kill you."'

'It's probably the couple who run the shop next door,' he said. 'They're always quarrelling. Their back shop is on the other side of our backyard and voices carry.'

'Oh,' said Agatha, a little disappointed that what had sounded like an intriguing mystery was only a marital quarrel. 'Are you married yourself?'

'I was once,' said Mr John. Those incredibly blue eyes of his glittered with humour. 'Didn't last long. Now I am free to enjoy the company of beautiful women. Speaking of which, when are you going to have dinner with me?'

'Tonight,' said Agatha, confident that he would not be free to make it.

'Tonight's fine,' he said. 'Give me your address and I'll pick you up at eight.'

He put down his scissors and reached for a

27

notepad. Agatha told him where she lived and he wrote it down. Agatha began to feel as nervous as a teenager. Would he expect her to have sex with him? She surreptitiously glanced at her wristwatch. She would be home before the salon closed. She could always phone and say something had come up.

But when her hair was blow-dried into a simple shorter style she felt a wave of gratitude for this magician.

And when she got home and felt the silence, the loneliness of the cottage settling round her, as suffocating as the humid heat, she decided that she would be mad to throw away the chance of dinner with a handsome man.

If the climate had changed, thought Agatha, and hot summers were going to become the norm, she would need to think about getting air-conditioning. She had read that to install air-conditioning cost twenty thousand pounds. It was two thousand for a portable unit. The last time she had visited America, she had noticed air-conditioners sticking out of windows of ordinary houses. Surely the average American family could not afford, say, thirty thousand dollars for air-conditioning or even three thousand for a portable unit.

Her cats lay stretched out on the kitchen floor, lethargic in the heat. She sat down on the floor next to them and stroked their warm fur. Where was James Lacey, and would he ever come back again?

She was flooded with such yearning that she let out a small moan. Depression settled down on her once more.

She sat there miserably until a glance at the clock showed her that she would need to hurry if she was to be ready on time.

*   *   *

Mr John took her to a French restaurant in the village of Blockley, which was only a few miles from Carsely.

'I still can't understand why an expert like you should settle for Evesham of all places,' said Agatha. 'You are good enough to compete with the best in London.'

'What's wrong with Evesham?' he teased. 'Evesham is the cradle of democracy.'

'How come?'

'Well, Simon de Montfort.'

Agatha looked blank.

'Don't tell me you've never heard of Simon de Montfort, Earl of Leicester!'

'No,' said Agatha with all the irritation one feels on being made to feel ignorant of historical facts, or any facts, for that matter.

'You've heard of King John and the Magna Carta?'

'Yes, got that at school.'

'It was to curb the power of the king. It

29

didn't really work. Both John and his son, Henry the Third, broke the charter whenever they could and only adhered to it when the barons threatened and complained. So they had to find a better way of making the king keep his word. In 1258, King Henry agreed to the Provisions of Oxford, which set up a permanent council to supervise his actions.

'Anyway, Henry paid as little attention to the Provisions of Oxford as John had paid to the Magna Carta. Simon, with the barons, decided to impose control. In 1264 there was a civil war. The king's army was beaten at Lewes in Sussex. Henry was taken prisoner along with his son, Edward.

'Simon called an emergency parliament of not only barons, but bishops and abbots, two knights from each shire and burgesses from a number of towns. He hoped to make it a lasting establishment.'

He paused to eat a piece of sea bass.

'What happened then?' asked Agatha. The story was keeping her mind off thoughts of James Lacey.

'Simon's support began to crumble. The Marcher lords from the borders of Wales rose against him and were joined by Gilbert de Clare, the young and powerful Earl of Gloucester. Simon led an army to the Severn, taking the king and Prince Edward with him as hostages, but the prince escaped at Hereford to lead the royalist uprising.

'Both forces converged on Evesham as Simon was preparing to enter the town. Simon's troops were massacred. Simon was beheaded and the head sent to his widow. His arms and legs and, erm, private parts were cut off. All that remained was the torso, which was buried at Evesham Abbey.'

'That's interesting,' said Agatha. 'Is his grave in the churchyard?'

'There's a memorial stone, but that's all. No one knows what happened to his remains. You see, people began to make pilgrimages to his grave to pay their respects to the "good Earl Simon". Rumour has it that the remains were dug up, burnt, and the ashes scattered to prevent worship of this dangerous democrat. The curator at the Almonry—the Evesham museum—he thinks Henry the Eighth was responsible, because a lot of the relics at Evesham Abbey were destroyed during the dissolution of the monasteries. Am I boring you?'

'No, I didn't know all this. I'd better take a closer look at Evesham.'

'So tell me all about yourself and your love life.'

They had drunk one bottle of wine and he had ordered another. Agatha, now slightly tipsy, found herself telling him all about James and about her brief fling with Charles. But she did not tell him that James knew all about Charles.

31

'So where is James now?'

'I don't know,' said Agatha sadly. 'Abroad somewhere.'

'You're an attractive woman.' He reached across the table and took her hand in his.

Agatha laughed and disengaged her hand. 'You make women feel attractive.'

'Tell me more about yourself.'

Agatha talked on but mostly about her days in public relations. Somehow the fact that Bill Wong hadn't phoned her hurt and so she did not brag about her detective abilities or mention his name.

And while she talked she began to wonder whether he would want to stay the night and whether she would let him. By the end of the meal she was languorously tipsy and was planning to invite him in when they got home.

As they left the restaurant, which was attached to the Crown Inn, Agatha saw Mrs Friendly emerging from the adjoining bar. 'Mrs Friendly,' called Agatha.

Mrs Friendly stood stock-still. Her eyes were wide with fright and her face paper-white as she looked at Mr John. She made an inarticulate sound and turned and went hurriedly back into the bar, pushing her way through people until she was lost to view.

Outside, Agatha said, 'You frightened her.'

'Who?'

'Mrs Friendly.'

'Who's she? Sounds like Happy Families.

Miss Bun, the Baker's Daughter, Mrs Friendly, the—'

'No, no. She was really frightened. The woman who was staring at you just as we left.'

'I saw no one I know. The restaurant behind us was crowded, Agatha. She probably saw someone behind us.'

Tipsy as she was, a little warning bell was beginning to sound in Agatha's brain. She had talked a lot about herself, but she knew practically nothing about this hairdresser apart from the fact that he possessed a good knowledge of Evesham history.

'Should you be driving?' she asked. 'We've had rather a lot to drink.'

'I've a hard head. Don't worry.'

'If you're sure. The fact that I know a lot of the police won't help us if we're caught.'

But he had marched ahead of her to the car and did not hear her.

When they reached her cottage and got out, Agatha turned to him and said firmly, 'Thank you so much for a delightful evening.'

'Aren't you going to ask me in?'

'Not tonight. I've had too much to drink. The next dinner's on me.'

'I'll keep you to that.' He bent to kiss her. Mrs Friendly's frightened face rose up in Agatha's mind and she turned her face so that his kiss landed on her cheek. 'Goodnight,' she said hurriedly and left him standing by the car, looking after her.

Agatha pottered about her house and garden the following day. It had rained during the night but the day was once more hot and stifling. The newspapers reported it was the hottest August in England since records had begun. There seemed to be a plague of mosquitoes and the Cotswold spiders were everywhere. Agatha did not like killing spiders and scooped the beasts up in kitchen paper and threw them out into the garden. One was descending from the kitchen ceiling in front of her eyes. She glared at it and it hurriedly retreated upwards, almost as if it were hauling itself up hand over hand.

She was wearing a washed-out cotton caftan she had bought years ago, with nothing underneath. On the kitchen floor, still in its box, was an electric fan she had bought in Evesham. She sighed. She tore open the box and lifted it out. It was in pieces. Did nothing come whole these days? She read the instructions carefully but could not unscrew one piece so as to attach the fan. She was just about to kick the infuriating thing across the floor when the doorbell rang.

Would she ever stop going to answer the door without hoping with all her heart that when she opened it James Lacey would be standing on the doorstep?

But it was Charles who stood there, looking cool and barbered.

'Come in,' said Agatha, her voice curt with disappointment. 'What brings you?'

'Got bored.' He followed her into the kitchen.

'You can make yourself useful. I can't put that fan together.'

'Make us a cup of coffee and I'll do it.'

Charles worked away busily at the large pedestal fan. 'Have you got one of those screwdrivers with the little cross at the head, Aggie?'

'In that box on the kitchen table. How do you want your coffee?'

'As ever. Milk, no sugar. If you loved me, Aggie, you would remember.'

'There's your coffee, Charles. I'm going upstairs to put some clothes on.'

Agatha went upstairs, took a quick shower, towelled and dressed in shorts and a cotton top.

When she went back to the kitchen, the fan was spinning busily.

'How clever of you, Charles,' said Agatha. 'What a relief! How did you get that big screw undone?'

'You unscrew it clockwise.'

'Now, how was anyone supposed to know that?' Agatha sat down at the kitchen table. 'I may have stumbled across a mystery, Charles.'

'What bleeding body have you tripped

over?'

'No body.' She told him about overhearing the pleading woman while she was in the toilet at the hairdresser's. 'Then I went out with this Mr John for dinner and as we were leaving, we ran into Mrs Friendly.'

'Who is she?'

'Newcomer to Carsely. Arrived last winter. Has one of those little cottages opposite the church. Mr John said she must have been looking at someone in the restaurant behind us but I'll swear it was him she was frightened of.'

'Is there a Mr Friendly?'

'Yes, he's a building contractor.'

'Do you think this hairdresser could have got his leg over, or maybe he's indulging in a spot of blackmail?'

Agatha's eyes gleamed. 'I thought of blackmail. The way women talk to their hairdressers! You should hear them.'

'Let's go and see this Mrs Friendly.'

Agatha shifted uneasily. 'What? Now?'

'Why not? Don't beat about the bush. Ask her why she was so frightened.'

'Shouldn't I phone first?'

'Let's surprise her.'

'All right,' said Agatha reluctantly. 'I'll put the cats out in the garden and lock up.'

* * *

36

Mrs Friendly's cottage was small and neat, two-storeyed, with no garden at the front.

They rang the bell. The door was opened by a very hairy man. He was wearing a tank top and shorts and grizzled hair sprouted all over his body. He had tufts of hair in his ears and hair sprouting out of his nose. His eyes were surprisingly weak and pale, peering at them from out of all this hairy virility. He must have been nearly sixty and Agatha thought he looked thoroughly unpleasant.

Agatha introduced herself and Charles and said they had called to see Mrs Friendly.

'Why?' His voice was thin and high.

'Ladies' Society.'

'Come in,' he said reluctantly.

The little cottage was dark and stifling. It had the original leaded windows, which looked so quaint and pretty from outside but allowed very little light to penetrate the inside. Mr Friendly ushered them into a hot, dark living room and said, 'I'll get Liza.'

'I didn't know he was retired,' whispered Agatha. 'Looks as if he must be.'

Fierce whispers were coming from the nether regions, then Mr Friendly's voice, sharp and angry: 'Just get rid of them.'

'Oh, dear,' muttered Agatha.

Liza Friendly came in. She had a round pleasant face, pretty even in middle age.

'Is it about the concert?' she asked.

'Not really,' said Agatha. 'I was at that

French restaurant in Blockley last night with Mr John and you saw us and I thought you look frightened.'

For one brief moment, Liza looked every bit as frightened as she had been the night before, but then she said brightly, 'Oh, I must have looked odd. It was the heat. I had to get out of there. I thought I was going to faint. Anything else?'

'Well, no,' said Agatha.

Liza had remained standing. She moved towards the door. 'In that case, I won't keep you.'

There was nothing else they could do but leave. 'I haven't introduced my friend,' said Agatha. 'Sir Charles Fraith.'

But Liza had reached the front door and was holding it open.

'Goodbye,' she said formally. 'How kind of you to call.'

'Well, that was a wash-out,' said Charles. 'Let's go back to your place and talk.'

They returned to the kitchen of Agatha's cottage. Agatha switched on the fan and poured two more cups of coffee.

'Now,' said Charles, 'if he's a blackmailer, there is one way to find out.'

'How?'

'You think of some truly awful secret, Aggie, and take him out for dinner and cry on his shoulder. Then we'll wait and see.'

'I could do that,' said Agatha slowly. 'You

know, we could be imagining things. Maybe she's just frightened of her hairy husband. Wait a bit. At the ladies' society meeting, I said I was going to Mr John in Evesham and she said something like, "I wouldn't go there." Oh, and there's something else. I did ask Mr John about those voices I overheard when I was in the toilet, but he said it was a husband and wife who owned the shop next door and who were always quarrelling. Should we watch Mrs Friendly's cottage and see if her husband goes out?'

'I think we should try my way first,' said Charles. 'Let's go somewhere for lunch and then I'll take a look at this hairdresser's in Evesham. You could make another appointment. Your hair looks nice like that.'

'Thank you. Where shall we have lunch?'

'Your choice.'

'I don't lunch in Evesham, but there's bound to be somewhere.'

They got into Charles's car and drove up through the hot countryside to the A44. 'You'd best cut off at the top of Fish Hill and go through Willersley,' said Agatha.

'Why?'

'It's the new Broadway by-pass they're building. There're traffic lights at the bottom of Fish Hill and you can get stuck there for ages.'

'Right you are.'

In Evesham and following Agatha's

39

directions, Charles parked at the top of the multi-storey car park next to the river Avon. They left the car and walked to Bridge Street. 'That looks all right.' Agatha pointed to a restaurant called the Lantern.

'I hope they do good chips,' said Charles, holding the door open for her. 'I like chips.'

The chips turned out to be real ones and not the frozen variety. 'Now what am I going to tell Mr John?' asked Agatha.

'Don't rush it. Wait till you get him out for dinner. I'll bet you told him about James.'

Agatha blushed guiltily.

'Ah, I thought so. Let me see. I know, James is due back but you've been having an affair with me.'

Agatha stared at the table.

'Oho, you gabby thing. You told him about me, too. He does have a way of winkling out secrets.'

'I didn't tell him that James had found out about us,' mumbled Agatha.

'There we have it. You want to marry James. He's a violently jealous man. He's written to say he loves you. You are terrified he finds out about me because *I* am violent and jealous.'

'I could do that,' said Agatha. 'I'm not normally so gossipy. It's just I seemed to have drunk quite a lot.'

'Did he try to go to bed with you?'

'He did expect to be asked in. No, Charles.

40

I am not amoral like you. I shall tell him I am keeping myself pure for James.'

'Good girl.'

They finished their meal and walked up Bridge Street and turned into the High Street.

'Look at that beautiful house,' said Charles, pointing across the road.

'It's a Chinese restaurant,' said Agatha. 'The Evesham Diner. Pretty good.'

'I don't care if it's pretty good. What kind of barbarians are there in this town not to preserve that lovely building properly? Look, here's a newsagent's. I'm going to buy a guidebook.'

Agatha sighed. The sun was beating down and the humidity had made her make-up melt.

Charles emerged with a small guidebook. 'Here we are. Dresden House. Built in 1692— see, I was right about William and Mary—by a Worcester man, Robert Cookes.'

'Why Dresden?'

'Ah, one owner of the house, Dr William Baylies, ran into financial trouble and went to live in Dresden, becoming physician to Frederick the Great of Prussia.'

'Never mind history. Here's the hairdresser. Oh, rats!'

'What rats?'

'I forgot, it's Wednesday. Half day. They're closed and I was all geared up with my story.'

'Come on, Aggie, you can't have been. Were you meaning to go in and make an

41

appointment and then say, "Oh, by the way, James is coming home and I'm having an affair with Charles here"?'

'I only meant I was all geared up to ask him out for dinner.'

'We'll trot about. Isn't there an abbey? What does the guidebook say? Ah, there was an abbey built in 700 AD but Henry the Eighth got rid of it. There's a museum in the old Almonry.'

'You're as bad as the hairdresser,' grumbled Agatha. 'I got a whole lecture on Simon de Montfort.'

'Then seduce him with your superior knowledge.'

The Almonry, where the almoner, the medical-social worker of his day, helped the less fortunate of the town, is a rambling fourteenth-century building.

Agatha and Charles went in. Agatha paid the entrance fee, for Charles took so long finding any money—deliberately, Agatha thought. Evesham is twinned with Dreux in France, where Simon de Montfort was born. They studied the charter proclaiming that fact. 'Heard about Stow-in-the-Wold?' asked Charles.

'No, what?'

'Some nice little town on the Loire wanted to be twinned with Stow, so the parish council put the vote to the townspeople and got a resounding NO.'

'Why?'

'Didn't want anything to do with the French. Can you believe it? They must still be fighting the battle of Waterloo over there.'

'So who did they decide to twin with?'

'Nobody. They're going to have a drinking fountain instead. I say, look at this map of the world, Aggie—1392, can you believe it?'

Agatha sighed. The heat was suffocating and she longed for a cigarette.

'Evesham is also twinned with Melsungen in Germany and Evesham, New Jersey.'

'Yawn,' said Agatha. 'Can't I go and sit in the garden and wait for you?'

'No, there's more upstairs. Come on.'

Agatha found herself becoming fascinated with two examples of Victorian dress. Usually in museums the ladies' shoes were tiny, but these Evesham ladies had great big feet.

They moved on. Agatha became uneasy as she saw household items she remembered from her youth.

She was relieved when the tour was over. But then Charles wanted to see the two churches, St Lawrence and All Saints. She fretted behind him wondering how such a frivolous man could become so excited over the sight of a Norman arch. Then they walked through the dark arch of the old Bell Tower, built between 1529 and 1539, chattered Charles, and so across the grass and down towards the river Avon. Just before the river was a paddling pool shrill with the cries of children. 'That's where the monks used to fish,' said Charles.

'Let's sit down for a moment,' said Agatha wearily.

They sat down together on a bench. It was a lazy, sunny scene. A band was churning out selections from *My Fair Lady*. Families sprawled on the grass. It looked so safe, so English, so far from the violence of the inner cities. Agatha relaxed. Evesham had a laid-back charm.

'Let's take a boat,' said Charles.

'Are you going to row?'

'Too hot. One of those pleasure boats.'

They walked back out into Bridge Street, past the multi-storey car park and so down to the landing stage, where a boat was just about to leave.

The boat went under the Workman Bridge and circled back when it came to a weir, then went back under the bridge and slowly along beside the Abbey Gardens, as they are called.

'Do you know that Evesham Abbey was larger than Gloucester Cathedral?' said Charles.

'Um,' said Agatha absently.

'And do you know that—What?' For Agatha had suddenly clutched his arm.

'Over there. Mr John,' hissed Agatha.

The open pleasure boat was sliding slowly past a tea garden. Charles looked. 'Blond

44

chap? Who's that with him?'

Agatha twisted her head backwards as the boat moved on. 'Don't know. Oh, yes. I think it's a customer of his called Maggie. We're all first names at the hairdresser's.'

'She didn't look all that happy.'

'We go back this way again, don't we?'

'Shortly, I should think. The trips are only half an hour long, so we should be turning back any moment now.'

Sure enough, the boat soon made a circle.

'Get ready,' said Agatha. 'Be prepared for a good look at them this time.'

But as the boat passed the tea garden, the table at which Mr John had been sitting with Maggie was empty.

'Pity,' said Agatha. 'She was bitching to him about how her husband didn't appreciate her. Do you think it really is blackmail? He might just be a philanderer.'

'So why was Mrs Friendly so frightened?'

'I'd forgotten about Mrs Friendly. I'll ask Mrs Bloxby, the vicar's wife. She might know something. Want to come with me?'

He looked at his watch. 'Can't. Got to get home soon. Going out tonight.'

'Where?'

'Taking this girl to see *Macbeth* at Stratford.'

'Oh,' said Agatha in a small voice. She felt disappointed but reminded herself that Charles was a bachelor with his own life to lead.

When they left the boat and walked back towards the car park, the heat was suffocating.

'Thunder tonight,' said Charles as they drove out of Evesham. Agatha looked ahead. There were purple clouds building up over Fish Hill.

'There's a thunderstorm almost every night,' she said, 'and yet the next day is always as hot and humid as ever.'

Charles grunted by way of reply. He seemed immersed in his own thoughts. Agatha could feel the edges of that depression in her brain. She would go and see Mrs Bloxby. Perhaps that would take up some of the lonely evening ahead.

When Charles dropped her off, he did not say anything about seeing her again. Agatha had a feeling that the mystery of the hairdresser had become a bore. She said goodbye to him in a subdued voice and let herself into her cottage just as the first fat raindrops struck the thatch on the roof.

She hurried to let her cats in and then opened a can of cat food for them. Her cats, Hodge and Boswell, although they purred around her ankles, seemed so self-sufficient, so little in need of the company of Agatha Raisin.

A blinding flash of lightning lit up the kitchen. Then came a crack of thunder which seemed to rock the old cottage to its very foundations. Agatha switched on the kitchen light only to find out that Carsely was suffering from one of the village's many power cuts.

She crept up to her bedroom and into bed without undressing, pulled the sheet over her and lay listening to the fury of the storm. She fell into an uneasy sleep, waking at seven in the evening feeling hot and gritty. Late sunlight streamed in at the windows.

She climbed out of bed and looked out of the window. Everything in the garden glittered in the sunlight. She leaned out. The air was as warm and sticky as ever.

Agatha showered and changed and then made her way along to the vicarage.

She hesitated on the doorstep as she heard the vicar's angry voice, 'Does that woman never think to phone first?'

She was about to turn away. That was the trouble with true Christians like Mrs Bloxby; one never thought of them as having any life of their own.

But the door opened and Mrs Bloxby smiled a welcome, pushing a wisp of grey hair out of her eyes.

'I saw you coming up the road,' she said. 'Come in.'

'And so did your husband,' said Agatha ruefully. 'He's quite right. I should have phoned first.'

'Never mind him. The heat is making us all

irritable and he's got evening service.'

'In that case . . .'

Agatha allowed herself to be led indoors just as the back door slammed angrily and through the window she could see the vicar striding off through the churchyard.

'The trouble is,' said Agatha, sitting down in the pleasant living room, 'that when something is bothering me, I simply come along to see you without thinking you might be busy.'

'It works both ways,' said Mrs Bloxby placidly. 'I never bother calling you first. I'll make some tea and then we'll have it in the garden and see if we can get a breath of air.'

She never fussed, thought Agatha enviously, as through the window she watched Mrs Bloxby wiping the raindrops from the garden table and chairs. Then she retreated to the kitchen to make tea before summoning Agatha into the garden.

'Look at that!' said Agatha. 'Over at the churchyard. The gravestones are actually steaming in the heat. Looks like some Dracula film.'

'We're heading towards the end of the month. The cooler weather should be here soon,' said Mrs Bloxby, pouring tea. 'Now, what is the matter? James?'

'No, it's my hairdresser.' Agatha told of her suspicions and Charles's idea of setting a trap.

'It could be quite dangerous for you.'

48

Mrs Bloxby's large grey eyes looked concerned. 'Surely this Mr John has heard of your reputation as a detective.'

'He remembers about my husband's murder. But I have never been credited in the newspapers with solving anything,' said Agatha. 'The credit has always gone to the police. Tell me about the Friendlys.'

'They haven't been in Carsely long, as you know. Let me see, there *was* some scene after morning service a few weeks ago. Alf told me.' Alf was the vicar.

'Alf had been preaching a sermon about how we should have minds above material things and Mr Friendly said something afterwards in the church porch about how he hoped his wife had been paying attention to the sermon because she was going through money like water. Mrs Friendly protested she had only been buying a few clothes and her husband said something like, "What clothes? I haven't noticed."'

'You think I should leave it alone?'

'One part of me thinks you should. On the other hand, it would be quite dreadful should he prove to be a blackmailer. Just think of the misery he would cause! But why not tell your friend, Bill Wong?'

'I can't,' said Agatha. 'Bill's on holiday.' She was still hurt by Bill's not phoning her and did not want to say that Bill was holidaying at home.

49

'What about his boss, Wilkes?'

'He thinks I'm an interfering pain. No, I would need proof. There's no harm in trying. At the worst he's going to blackmail me. Not kill me.'

'So what do you plan to do?'

'I meant to ask him out but think I'll make a hair appointment and this time watch and listen. See if I can suss out any other customers he might be putting the squeeze on.'

'Be careful. Now about the concert at Ancombe. It's very good of you to take over the catering. Do you want me to help you?'

'No, I'll manage.' Agatha had already decided to hire a catering firm to make cakes and savouries. Worth every penny to put Mrs Darry's nose out of joint.

'You know, I'm beginning to wish I had never recommended Mr John. But he has such a good reputation. Mrs Jessie Black over at Ancombe, the chairwoman of the ladies' society, she used to sport a terrible frizzy perm in an impossible shade of red and he tinted it auburn and put it into a beautifully smooth style.'

'I'll see if I can get an appointment,' said Agatha. 'I'll try tomorrow.'

*   *   *

Agatha made her way to Evesham. The old

buildings of Evesham shimmered in the dreadful heat. She parked in the car park although she would have liked to try to find a parking place outside the hairdresser's but did not want another confrontation with some embittered local.

Alert now for nuances, Agatha noticed this time that the receptionist, a vapid blonde in a pink overall with her name, Josie, on a badge on her left breast, gave her a sour, jealous look.

'I was certainly lucky to get a cancellation,' said Agatha brightly.

'Yes,' said Josie, jerking a pink gown round Agatha's shoulders. 'Mr John is particularly popular with the elderly.'

'Was that crack meant for me?' demanded Agatha, rounding on her savagely.

'Oh, no, modom.' Josie backed away, flustered. 'I'll just get Yvette to shampoo you.'

Ruffled, Agatha sat down at a wash-basin and looked around. From the adjoining area, she could hear a woman's voice raised in complaint. 'I can't do anything with her these days. I said, "That stuff'll kill you," and she says to me, "Heroin is my friend." My own daughter on drugs! The shame of it. My neighbour says she thinks my Betty is pushing the stuff.'

'Can't your husband have a word with her?' came Mr John's voice.

'Jim? Him! He doesn't know she's on the

stuff and he wouldn't believe me even if I told him. Betty's always been able to twist him round her little finger. Daddy's girl. Always been daddy's girl.'

Yvette arrived and put a towel around Agatha's neck. The subsequent hissing of the water drowned out the rest of the conversation between Mr John and his customer.

A hairdresser's salon is like the psychiatrist's couch, reflected Agatha. The things they talk about. Didn't that woman stop to think that one of the other customers might hear her and report her daughter to the police? But no. Hairdressers and beauty salons were like the confessional. The only one liable to profit from all these confidences was the hairdresser himself.

Agatha had her hair towelled and was led through to the salon where Mr John flashed her a smile. Josie brought him a cup of coffee in a Styrofoam container and he added two pills of artificial sweetener called Slimtex. 'I get my coffee sent in from across the road,' he said. 'It's that caff over there. Bit seedy, but they make marvellous coffee. Now, Agatha, let's put you back together again.'

Agatha sighed. 'I don't see how you can do much in this heat. It's worse than rain.'

'We'll try.'

He rested his hands on her shoulders and gave them a light press.

'I owe you a dinner,' said Agatha.

'So you do and I'm going to keep you to it.'

Agatha took a deep breath. 'Are you free tonight?'

'As a matter of fact, I am.'

'Oh. Oh, well, shall I pick you up?'

'No, I'll call for you at eight. Josie, what are you doing standing there with your mouth hanging open? The phone's ringing.'

Josie fled. Mr John shrugged. 'Young girls these days,' he murmured.

Agatha's hair was restored to a glossy, smooth shine. When she left the hairdresser's, she walked quickly to the car park, hoping she would not sweat too much and ruin the set.

When she got home, she debated whether she should phone Charles. But she felt sulky. He had said nothing about seeing her again. He seemed to walk in and out of her life, expecting her to be available.

*   *   *

She dressed with care but unfortunately not for comfort. She had read that stiletto heels were back in fashion and so had bought a gold sling-back pair, proud of the fact that she still had strong enough ankles to wear such high heels. But the heat had softened her skin and the criss-cross straps on the top of her shoes dug uncomfortably into her feet.

She decided that as she would be sitting in

his car and then sitting in some restaurant or other, she could bear it. Just before he arrived, she slipped a little tape recorder into her handbag.

Mrs Darry was walking her yapping little dog down Lilac Lane as Agatha was escorted to the car by Mr John. Agatha flashed her a triumphant look, delighted that the village bitch should witness her going out for the evening with such a handsome man. But Mrs Darry, instead of stopping and staring rudely, as she usually did, took to her heels and scurried off down the lane, dragging her protesting dog after her.

'Where are we going?' asked Agatha.

'The Marsh Goose in Moreton.'

'Nice,' said Agatha but reflected gloomily that there was no smoking except in the coffee lounge. It was odd that people who did not drink could never somehow say, 'Don't drink in front of me,' but smokers were always made to feel guilty. Three scientists had recently issued a report that you were more in danger of getting cancer from eating dairy products than you were from passive smoking because dairy products were a killer, but smoking brought out the puritanical beast in people. By the time she reached the restaurant, she craved a cigarette, but did not dare say so.

She put her handbag on her lap, opened it and covertly switched on the tape recorder. Then she switched it off again. A noisy party

54

of people were at the next table, making conversation between her and the hairdresser almost impossible.

To her relief, the noisy party finally left. Agatha switched on the tape recorder again and turned a dewy-eyed look on Mr John. 'It's such a break from my troubles to have a quiet dinner like this with you.'

'What troubles, Agatha?' He reached across the table and took her hand.

'It's James,' said Agatha. To her horror, her eyes filled with tears.

Mr John's thumb caressed the palm of her hand. 'Tell me about it.'

'He's coming home, and I've missed him so much. I've been having an affair with Charles.'

'The baronet?'

'Yes, him. Charles is violently jealous. I tried to finish with him. He says he won't go away. I'm frightened James will get to hear about it. I'd do anything—anything—to stop him finding out.'

He asked more questions and the more Agatha began to build up a picture of a violent and jealous Charles, the more she began almost to believe it.

But by the time she had moved through with Mr John to the lounge for coffee, she realized she had done all the talking. She drew out a packet of cigarettes.

'That's a filthy habit, Agatha. Do you mind if I ask you not to smoke?'

'Yes, I mind very much,' snapped Agatha.

'You're killing yourself.'

'And so is everyone like you who drives a car that belts carcinogens into the air.'

Agatha then hurriedly closed her handbag, which she had opened wide in her search for cigarettes. She hoped he had not seen the tape recorder. Anyway, he was surely not going to blackmail her tonight.

He began to talk easily about how successful his business in Evesham had proved to be and that he was thinking of opening up another salon. 'It's war, hairdressing,' he said with a laugh. 'It's like the theatre. You would never believe the rivalries and jealousies. And I'm thinking of starting up a beauty salon.'

Agatha fumbled in her handbag and switched off the tape recorder. She felt heavy and sad. And her feet were killing her.

At last she said, 'It's been nice. Do you mind if we go home?' She signalled to the waiter and asked for the bill. 'My treat, remember?'

'You're looking tired,' he said, his blue eyes full of concern.

He drove a silent Agatha home. He helped her out of the car and then said, 'I would really like to see the inside of your cottage.'

Agatha was wearily thinking of polite excuses when a wrathful voice behind her made her jump.

'And just who the hell is this, Aggie!'

56

Chapter Three

Charles stood there, his hands clenched into fists at his side. At first, Agatha was too taken aback to realize it was an act.

'I've been out for dinner with John,' she said. 'Charles, may I introduce you? This is—'

'I don't want to meet scum like this.' Charles seized her arm and jerked her towards him. Her clutch handbag went spinning and the contents spilled out over the road, exposed in the security lights which had come on in the front of Agatha's cottage. Her little black tape recorder went flying across the cobbled surface of the road and landed at Mr John's feet.

He picked it up. Charles stood frozen, his hand on Agatha's arm.

'Yours, I think.' Mr John held out the tape recorder to Agatha, who numbly took it. His eyes glittered with malice and amusement.

Then he waved his hand and got into his car and roared off.

Agatha rounded on Charles. 'What the hell were you playing at?' She stooped and began to gather up the contents of her bag.

'I was just playing my part,' said Charles mildly. 'I went to the Red Lion and learned you were off with Mr John. So I decided to hang about until you came home and play the

57

jealous lover.'

'Why didn't you tell me?'

'I couldn't. I didn't know what you were up to. Why didn't you phone me? I thought we were in this together.'

'Oh, come into the house. I'm fed up. He saw the tape recorder, so he's wise to us.'

He followed her into the house and through to the kitchen. 'Maybe not.'

'Why not?' demanded Agatha, angrily plugging in the kettle. 'I saw the expression in his eyes when he handed me that tape recorder.'

'Well, he knows you were in publicity. Lots of people carry those little tape recorders around. I sometimes carry one myself to remind me of appointments and things to do.'

'A blackmailer is not going to think that,' jeered Agatha.

'We don't know he's a blackmailer. Make me a coffee while I think. Give me a cigarette.'

'You don't smoke.'

'I only smoke other people's. It's a charitable gesture. It reduces their intake.'

'And stops you spending the money yourself. Cheapskate! Oh, help yourself. There's a packet in my handbag.'

Agatha made two cups of instant coffee. She had given up making fresh coffee and was back to microwaving most of her meals. Old habits refused to die. She was weary of trying to be 'a village person'.

'What can we possibly do now?' she asked, sitting down at the table.

'I'm thinking. Let's assume he *is* a blackmailer. Why does one become a blackmailer?'

'Power?'

'But money must be a strong motive. Money and greed. Think about this one. If you were to give him an expensive present. Drop the James business. Glow at him. Let him think he's the one.'

'What present?' asked Agatha suspiciously.

'Little something from Asprey's. Does he smoke?'

'No, not even mine.'

'What about a tasteful pair of solid-gold cuff-links in a dinky little Asprey box?'

'What about spending a thousand pounds? Are you going to contribute?'

He looked shifty and his hand instinctively clasped protectively over the breast of his jacket. The foreigner presses his heart, thought Agatha cynically, but your true blue-blooded Englishman presses his wallet to make sure it's safe.

'Why should I waste a lot of money on a provincial hairdresser?' Agatha demanded.

'Because,' said Charles patiently, 'it would keep the game going, and the reason for keeping the game going is you're bored.'

'And so are you,' said Agatha shrewdly.

'But not as bored and depressed and lovelorn as you, light of my life.'

'I'll think about it.'

'Do. You'll find he'll melt like butter and only think the best of you.'

'If you've finished your coffee, I'll show you out.'

'I'm tired. Can't I stay here?'

'No. Out.'

'Okay.' He got to his feet. 'Let me know how you get on.'

'I haven't said I'll do it.'

'Think about it, Aggie. Think about it.'

*　　*　　*

Charles was right. Agatha could not bear to drop what she was beginning to consider 'her case'.

She drove to Moreton-in-Marsh station early the next morning and joined the commuters on the platform. Then the woman who manned the ticket office came out and shouted, 'There will be no trains due to a shortage of engine drivers.'

Cursing, Agatha walked back over the iron bridge to the car park. She got in her car and drove to Oxford and took a train from there to Paddington. From Paddington, she took a taxi to Asprey's in Bond Street. In the almost religious hush of the great jeweller's, she examined trays of cuff-links, finally selecting a heavy, solid-gold pair and paying a price for them which left her feeling breathless.

She then travelled to the City to see her stockbroker and be reassured that her stocks and shares were prospering. As she was in the City, she called at Pedmans to see Roy Silver, a public relations officer who had originally worked for her before she had sold out to Pedmans.

'I haven't heard from you for a while,' said Agatha, reflecting that Roy looked as weedy and unhealthy as ever. But obviously he was doing well. Her practised eye noticed that his suit was Armani.

'I've been very busy, sweetie. How's life in Boresville?'

'I thought you liked the country. You're always saying how lucky I am.'

'A passing aberration. Sophisticates like me would wilt in the country.'

'You're joking, of course.'

'Not really. What are you doing anyway? Village fêtes?'

'No, much more exciting than that,' said Agatha, but remembered that she had to arrange the teas for Ancombe and had better get back and call a catering company.

'Murder?'

Agatha wanted to brag. 'I'm chasing a blackmailer.'

'Tell me about it.'

So Agatha did.

61

Roy was intrigued. 'Tell you what, I'll come down this weekend and help you.'

He hadn't bothered phoning her for a long time, so Agatha said huffily, 'Can't. I'm busy this weekend.'

*   *   *

When she got home, she phoned the hairdresser's and made an appointment for the day after the next. The following day was the concert at Ancombe. Then she phoned a top catering firm in Mircester and ordered sandwiches, cakes and hot savouries to be delivered to her early the following morning. Agatha meant to convey the goodies to the concert herself and produce them as her own.

On the following morning, she transferred all the catering firm's supplies into her own boxes and put them in the boot of her car and drove to Ancombe.

With the good excuse that she could not watch the concert because she would be too busy preparing the teas, she escaped into an adjoining hall where three schoolgirls had been drafted to help her put out the tables and chairs. The hall smelt like all church halls, dusty and redolent of dry rot and sweat. The church hall was not only used by the Scouts but by an aerobics class as well.

She could hear Miss Simms's voice raised in shrill song. If it was meant to be Cher, then it was a Cher in the process of getting liposuction.

Agatha heated trays of savouries in the oven and spread cakes and sandwiches on plates. It looked a magnificent feast.

Finally she heard the strains of 'God Save the Queen'—the Ancombe ladies were traditionalists—raised in song. Then there was the scraping back of chairs and they all came filing in, exclaiming in delight at the spread laid out for them.

But Mrs Darry was not amongst them. What a lot of money I do waste on pettiness, thought Agatha with a rare pang of remorse.

There was no Mrs Friendly either, so she could not even continue her investigation.

By the end of the event, she felt tired and sticky. Mrs Bloxby stayed behind to help Agatha load and stack empty foil trays in her car.

'You did us proud, Mrs Raisin,' said Mrs Bloxby. 'If you ever feel like going into business again, you could be a professional caterer.'

Agatha looked at her sharply and the vicar's wife gave her an innocent look. But Agatha knew she had been rumbled and felt silly.

For the first time in her life, she began to feel that living alone was an effort. Not that she had ever lived with anyone else, apart from a brief sojourn with James. If she lived with someone, then that someone would be there to chatter to her as she contemplated washing out the foil trays. After the catering company had called to pick up theirs, she reminded herself that the main purpose of foil trays was that they were disposable and put the whole lot in a rubbish bag.

The heat was suffocating. She wandered out into her garden. She had lost interest in gardening and hired a local man to do that. Mrs Simpson did her cleaning for her. Pity she couldn't hire someone to do the living for her. The gardener was not due to call for another two days, and despite the recent rain the flowers were beginning to wilt in the heat.

She got out the hose and went to fix it to the tap in the garden but sat down in a garden chair instead. The depression she had been fighting off all day engulfed her and immobilized her.

She sat there while the sun slowly sank in the sky and the trees at the end of the garden cast long shadows over the grass. The pursuit of money and success had been everything in her life. Money meant the best restaurants, security, the best medical attention if she fell ill, and, at the end of her days, a good old folks' home where they actually looked after the patients. She felt as if the tide of life had receded, leaving her stranded on a sandbank of money.

'I will not sink down under this,' she

muttered to herself. Feeling like an old woman, she rose from her chair and went to the garden shed and wheeled out her bicycle. Minutes later, she was cycling off down the country lanes, pedalling fast like one possessed, racing to leave that tired failure of an Agatha behind her.

She pedalled while darkness fell over the countryside and light came on in cottage windows. When she at last turned homewards and free-wheeled down the hill into Carsely under the arched tunnels made by the trees on either side of the road, she felt calm and exhausted.

She let the cats in from the garden, locked up for the night, made herself a ham sandwich, then showered and went to bed and fell into a deep sleep.

When Agatha awoke in the morning, she felt stiff and sore from the exercise, but prepared for the day ahead. She put the little Asprey's box in her handbag and drove to the hairdresser's. On the other side of Broadway she looked up at the sky. Mares' tails streamed across the blue of the sky. The weather must be about to change.

By the time she drove into Evesham, the sky was changing to grey. To her delight, there was actually a legal parking space right outside the hairdresser's.

With a twinge of apprehension, she opened the door and went in. With something like triumph, the receptionist informed her that Mr Garry would do her hair.

'Who the hell's Mr Garry?' snarled Agatha. 'And stop grinning when you speak to me.'

'Mr Garry is Mr John's assistant,' said the receptionist, Josie. Agatha was about to cancel her appointment, but she got a glimpse of herself in one of the many mirrors. Her hair looked limp and sweaty.

Yvette washed her hair and then she was led through to the ministrations of Mr Garry, who proved to be a youth who chattered endlessly about shows he had seen on television. Agatha interrupted the flow by asking, 'What's Mr John got?'

'He phoned in to say he was under the weather. He didn't say exactly what it was.'

'Does he live in Evesham?'

'Yes, one of those villas on the Cheltenham Road.'

Agatha's hair emerged as shiny and healthy as it had recently become, but she was unhappy with the style, which looked slightly rigid. Normally she would have complained and made him do it again, but she was tired of sitting in the hairdresser's. As she was paying for her hair-style, she saw a framed certificate behind the desk. So Mr John's second name was Shawpart.

She went along to the post office and asked for a phone book and found only one Shawpart. She took a note of the number in

Cheltenham Road and, swinging round into the traffic, headed in that direction. As she crossed the bridge over the river Avon, she noticed the water was greenish black and very still under a lowering sky.

Up the hill, past the garage, past the hospital and along in the direction of the by-pass she went, until she found Mr John's house, a fairly large modern villa. She parked outside and walked up the short path and rang the doorbell.

There was a long silence, broken only by the sound of the traffic humming past her on the road behind her. The sky above was growing even darker. Then she faintly heard the sound of shuffling footsteps, like those of a very old man.

She suddenly wished she had not come. The door swung open on the chain.

'Oh, it's you,' said Mr John's voice. 'Come in.'

He unlatched the chain and stood back. The hallway was in darkness. He led the way into a sitting-room and switched on a lamp and turned around.

Agatha let out an exclamation. His face was black with bruises.

'What on earth happened to you?' she asked. 'Car accident?'

'Yes, last night. Some drunken youth ran into me and I hit the windscreen.'

'Didn't you have an air bag? Or didn't you

67

have your seat-belt on?'

'I don't have one of those models with an air bag. I'd just started to drive off, so I didn't have a seat-belt on.'

'What did the police say?'

'I didn't bother reporting it. I mean, what could they do? I didn't get the number of the other car.'

'But you have to report it to the police! The insurance—'

'Oh, just leave it. I don't want to talk about it. What do you want?'

Agatha had planned to be flirtatious, but confronted with his black-and-blue face, she did not quite know how to begin.

'I heard you were ill,' she began, 'and was concerned about you.'

'That was nice of you.' He rallied himself with an effort. 'Can I offer you something? Tea? Something stronger?'

'No, don't trouble. How long have you lived here?'

'Why?'

Agatha blinked. 'Just wondered. Here.' She fumbled in her handbag. 'Just a silly little present I got you.' She handed him the Asprey's box.

He opened it and stared down at the heavy gold cuff-links nestling in their little bed of velvet.

Suddenly his face and manner were transformed. 'How beautiful. And how very,

very generous. I don't know what to say.'

He came across to her and bent down and kissed her on the cheek. 'Now, we really must have a drink to celebrate. No, we must. I insist.'

He went out and returned after a few moments carrying a bottle of champagne and two glasses. He expertly popped the cork, filled the glasses and handed one to Agatha.

Agatha raised her glass. 'Here's to friendship,' she said.

'Oh, I'll drink to that. I do need a friend.' His voice had a ring of sincerity for the first time. I wonder if I've been mistaken about him, thought Agatha.

He sat down and held his tulip glass in one slender hand. 'You were asking how long I had lived here? About a year. I had been working in Portsmouth and I wanted a change of scene. I saw in the *Hairdresser's Journal* that this business in Evesham was going for sale. When I first came to Evesham, I looked the place over. It seemed neither go-ahead, nor sophisticated. But there was something about the sheer laziness of the place which got to me. And I knew there were a lot of rich people in the surrounding villages. Well, the business took off almost from the beginning. Although I am thinking of moving on. I get restless after I've been in the same place for a bit.'

Agatha glanced around her at the heavy

furniture, and the dark wallpaper decorated with uninspiring scenes of the Cotswolds, those sort of scenes, peculiarly lifeless, painted by local artists as if they had meticulously copied photographs.

'Did you take this place furnished?'

'Yes, I rent it. Not my taste. So how's your muddled love life, Agatha?'

She manufactured a world-weary shrug. 'That scene Charles threw was the last straw. I'm weary of James.' She looked down at the floor and wished she could blush to order. 'I kept thinking about you, instead.'

'I've been thinking about you as well,' he said. 'We could make a great team.'

She looked at him in surprise.

He put his glass down and leaned forward. 'You wondered why I didn't move to London. Well, I've been thinking about it. One of my customers told me about how successful you were at organizing things and about your public relations job. Oh, I know you told me, but it was only later I thought of it. I've enough money put by to take a lease on a place in the centre of town, Knightsbridge, Sloane Street, somewhere near Harrods. With my hairdressing skills and your public relations skills, I could be another Vidal Sassoon.'

If only I could believe he was not a blackmailer, thought Agatha quickly. But string him along anyway.

'Do you know, that could be very exciting. I miss London. And it would get me out of the mess I've made for myself down here. When do we start?'

'It'll take some time to wind things up in Evesham. We could think about starting next year.'

He can't have thought that tape recorder meant anything, Agatha decided. She stood up. 'I really must be going. I'm sorry about your accident. When are you back at work?'

'Couple of days.'

'I'll make an appointment when I know you're going to be there.'

He surveyed her. 'Garry did that to you, didn't he?' She nodded. 'You see, that's the trouble. It's so hard to get assistants with any flair. Good hairdressers are born, not made.'

He walked with her to the door. 'When you come in for that appointment, we'll fix up a date for dinner.' He put an arm around her shoulders and gave her a squeeze. 'We're going to be a great partnership. I'm good at raising money, so funds won't be any problem.'

'I've got some money of my own. I could help you.'

He swept her into his arms and kissed her passionately. 'What did I ever do before I met you,' he said huskily.

Well, well, well, thought Agatha shakily as she made her way to her car. Perhaps I really was mistaken in him. He is rather a dish.

She decided to drive into Evesham and buy some groceries in case Charles wanted to come to dinner. She was tired of eating out.

The villa was on the corner of a side road. She drove round into the side road to make a three-point turn and so drive back into town. It was then she noticed Mr John's car at the side of the house, gleaming, unmarked.

Surely he could not have got it repaired so quickly. Did some jealous husband beat him up? Someone he had been blackmailing?

But that kiss still burned on Agatha's lips and she found she was becoming inclined to think that there was nothing wrong with him, except perhaps that he was a bit of a philanderer.

As she drove back into town and to Tesco's supermarket, she began to feel the first surge of excitement about his idea of starting a salon in London. She was a shrewd enough businesswoman to make certain it prospered. He certainly was talented, more talented than London hairdressers Agatha had gone to. She had only said that bit about putting her money into his business to get him on the hook and allay his suspicions that she was on to him.

But what if he was genuine? She could get out of Carsely and back into an exciting, busy life. James would return and find her gone. With work to do, she would not have time to think of him.

She drifted around the supermarket wondering what to get for dinner. Then she reflected it was silly to waste money on expensive food for Charles, who would probably prefer sausage, egg and chips to anything else.

She queued and paid for her groceries, all the time thinking of the hairdressing project as escape.

It was only when she finally entered her cottage and began to unpack her groceries that Agatha's common sense began to reassert itself. Mr John surely got women on the hook by being charming to them. And yet . . . and yet . . . If he had reason to suspect she was on to him, why offer her a business proposition where she would be working closely with him? He had not asked for any money. She had offered it. She phoned Charles and asked him for dinner, telling him she would let him know her news when he arrived.

The sad fact was that Agatha had become addicted to the state of being in love and was all too ready to transfer that love to someone, anyone, other than James Lacey.

*   *   *

Charles arrived just as the first crack of lightning split the sky overhead. 'Let's hope the weather's broken at last,' he said.

'Do you mind if we eat in the kitchen?' said

Agatha.

'Not at all. What delicacies are you going to microwave for me?'

'Sausage, egg and chips, all fried.'

'Good. I'd like a bit of fried bread as well.'

'You've got it. Go and make yourself a drink and get me a gin and tonic while I fry. I'll tell you all about it over dinner.'

Agatha turned to the stove. There was another great crack of thunder and then all the lights went out.

'Blast!' she shouted to Charles, who was at the drinks trolley in the living-room. 'I'll light candles. Don't fall over anything.'

She fumbled in the kitchen drawer for the candles she kept in readiness to cope with Carsely's many power cuts. Charles came in holding a branch of candles he had taken from the dining-room table. 'If you're all right, I'll go back and get the drinks.'

'Wait a bit. I've got a big torch in this cupboard under the sink.' Agatha found it and handed it to him.

He put the candles with the others on the kitchen table and retreated with the torch.

'Thank God this is a gas cooker,' muttered Agatha.

When dinner was cooked, they sat down to eat it in candle-light.

'Now,' said Charles, 'what happened?'

Agatha told him about her visit, about the hairdresser's bruised face, about the business offer and how she had found the car, unmarked, at the side of the house.

'So it does look as if someone might have beaten him up. Good,' remarked Charles.

Agatha said, 'I've been wondering if we've been wrong . . . about the blackmailing, I mean. Maybe he's just a ladies' man.'

'A successful one, too, by the look in your eyes. Agatha, he's after your money.'

'I offered it. All he was doing was offering me a job.'

'Which you wouldn't dream of accepting.'

'It might be a good idea. I mean, I'm *rotting* here in Carsely.'

'When you talked about your life in London, I always got the impression you were rotting there without knowing it. You've got friends here. Something always seems to be happening to you.'

'I could do it for a bit. See how it works. I wouldn't sell up here till I was sure.'

'Aggie, he *has* got to you, you silly old thing.'

Agatha winced at that 'old' but said defensively, 'In any case I mean to string him along. It's a good way of getting to know him better. Then I can be sure.'

'I think that's a damn dangerous thing to do.'

'Why? If he does try to blackmail me, then I'll go straight to the police.'

'Aggie, blackmailers create violence. You've

gone potty.'

But Agatha had begun to build a dream up in her head of being back working in London. Why not go for Bond Street? Start with a splash. Big party. Get all the celebs. She could practically smell the petrol fumes of Bond Street, the scent from the perfume counter at Fenwick's, the glowing pictures in the art galleries, the glittering jewels in Asprey's window.

And perhaps, just perhaps, if he kissed her again like that, the bright pictures of James would fade and die.

'If you don't want to know any more about it . . .' she began huffily.

'Oh, I do. I've a feeling you're going to need my help soon. Listen to that storm, Aggie. You're surely not going to send me home tonight.'

'You can sleep here . . . in the spare room.'

The phone rang. Agatha picked up the kitchen extension. It was Mr John, his voice warm and concerned. 'I just wanted to know you were all right.'

'Yes, I'm fine. Why?'

'This terrible storm. There are trees down everywhere. Have you electricity?'

'No, but I've a gas cooker and candles.'

'I'm very excited about our business project and would like to talk some more about it. Why don't you drop over here tomorrow afternoon at three, say?'

'Yes, I'd like that. Get off!' Charles had crept up behind her and kissed the back of her neck.

'What's going on?' demanded the hairdresser sharply. 'Who's there?'

'No one,' said Agatha. 'Just a mosquito. I'll see you tomorrow. Bye.'

She swung round on Charles. 'What did you do that for? That was John.'

'I guessed as much. You are getting into deep water, Aggie.'

'I'm not,' she protested huffily. She took a Sarah Lee apple pie out of the freezer and put it in the oven. 'I should have put that on earlier,' she said. 'Let's go and relax.'

As they went into the living-room, all the lights came on again. 'Good,' said Charles, 'we can watch telly.'

He switched it on and flicked the channels until he came across a rerun of *Hill Street Blues* and settled down happily to watch.

'You didn't even ask me if I wanted to see that,' said Agatha crossly. 'And it is my television set.'

'Shh!'

So they watched *Hill Street Blues* and then there was a Barbra Streisand movie and Charles was addicted to Barbra Streisand. While he watched, Agatha let dreams of a new life curl around her brain rather like the smoke which was beginning to curl under the kitchen door. She had forgotten about the apple pie and it was only as smoke began to drift between them and the television set that she realized with a squawk of alarm what had happened. She ran to the kitchen and switched off the oven and opened the door and windows. Sweet cool air drifted in. She walked out into the garden. The rain had stopped and a little chilly moon sailed overhead through ragged clouds. She stood breathing in the fresh air until all the smoke had cleared from the kitchen. The pie when she removed it was a blackened mess. She threw it into the wastebin and then began to diligently clean the surfaces of the kitchen.

By the time she had finished cleaning, the movie had ended and Charles was watching *Star Trek, The Next Generation*, an early one, to judge from the beardless and baby-faced Commander Riker.

'Charles,' said Agatha crossly. 'It's late and the storm's over. You can go home.'

'I haven't got Sky Television and I haven't seen this one.'

'Home, Charles.'

He left grumbling. 'I'll call you tomorrow,' he said, 'but you don't deserve my concern.'

*   *   *

The next day was almost chilly and the residents of Carsely, like the rest of the British Isles who had been bitching for weeks about the heat, began to bitch instead about the cold.

Agatha dressed carefully in a tailored suit and silk blouse and headed for Evesham. Her dreams of the day before had faded and would have stayed faded had John not immediately taken her in his arms when she arrived and given her another of those warm, passionate kisses full on the mouth.

She felt quite weak at the knees as she sat down. His bruises appeared to be fading fast and his eyes were as blue, as intensely blue, as ever.

'Have you thought any more about my business proposition?' he asked.

Agatha flexed her public relations muscles. She described how she thought they should go big from the word go, open in Bond Street, say. She outlined how she would go about rousing interest so she could get it into as many newspapers as possible. 'And do you know what we'll call it?'

'I thought just Mr John.'

'No, we'll call it the Wizard of Evesham.'

He looked at her thoughtfully and then began to laugh. 'I like that. It's catchy. I like it a lot.'

All afternoon, they talked busily. Then he sent out for Chinese food. Before dinner, he opened a bottle of pills and popped two in his mouth. 'Is that your medicine?' asked Agatha.

'No, they're vitamin pills, a multi-vitamin

called Lifex. I swear by them. I keep a supply in the shop. You should try them.'

Agatha picked up the bottle and shook one out. 'I'm not very good at swallowing pills,' she said, looking at the large brown gelatine capsule in her hand. 'I would choke on something this size. What do they do for you?'

'I find they give me a lot of energy. Let's eat.'

They talked busily over dinner, firing ideas for their new venture back and forth across the table. Agatha at last said reluctantly that she should get home.

If he had asked her to stay with him, Agatha probably would have succumbed, but he only gathered her back into his arms as he said goodnight and again sent her senses spinning with one of those kisses, fuelling the hopelessly romantic side of Agatha to boiling point.

She decided as she drove dreamily home that all her suspicions of him had been unfounded. What were they based on after all? One frightened village woman who had probably had a crush on him, had probably written him a silly love letter or something like that and her bad-tempered husband had found out.

There was a message from Charles on her Call Minder but she did not want to phone him, did not want anything to burst the rosy bubble in which she floated. Mr John—no,

John—stop calling him that silly hairdresser's name—had said he had taken the liberty of making an appointment for her for the following day. Soon she would see him again.

Agatha in love meant an Agatha who could not make up her mind what to wear. Although she started her preparations early the next day, she at last left in a rush, wearing a coat over a sweater and skirt and having torn off more dressy ensembles, feeling she looked as if she were trying too hard.

She would need to steer him to a good interior decorator, she thought, looking round the salon in a proprietorial way. And no receptionist like the dreadful Josie, but no one too glamorous either.

She was shampooed and with a dithering feeling of anticipation was led through to Mr John.

'Agatha,' he said, giving her a warm smile. He pressed her shoulders and then gripped them hard.

She looked, startled, at his reflection in the mirror. Under the bruises, his face was an unhealthy red colour.

'Excuse me,' he muttered. He fled to the toilet. The tape deck was playing a selection of sixties pop. The Beatles were belting out 'She's got a ticket to ride', filling the salon with noisy sound. The number finished and then Agatha and everyone else could hear retching sounds coming from the toilet.

81

Agatha went through and knocked at the door and called, 'What's the matter?'

Another bout of dreadful retching answered her. She was joined by the assistant, Garry.

'He sounds terribly ill,' said Agatha. She rattled the door handle.

'John! John! Let me in.'

She was answered by a loud tearing groan. Then crashing noises.

'Break open the door!' she shouted at Garry.

The willowy Garry threw himself against it but succeeded only in hurting his shoulder.

Agatha was joined by the other customers. Maggie was amongst them, she noticed.

'Get me a screwdriver or chisel,' said Agatha. 'Quick. Josie, phone for an ambulance.'

Garry went into the nether regions and came back with a tool-box. Agatha seized a chisel and stuck it into the door jamb at the lock and jerked it sideways. There was a splintering and cracking as the flimsy lock gave way.

Mr John was lying on the floor. He was now stretched out, immobile, his eyes staring upwards. His pale grey eyes. God, even his eyes have changed colour, thought Agatha wildly.

She knelt down and felt for his pulse, only finding a faint flutter. In the distance, she could hear the wail of the ambulance siren. Thank God, the hospital was quite near.

She gagged at the smell. Vomit was everywhere.

'Ambulance is here!' shouted Josie. Everyone except Agatha rushed to the door. She stared helplessly down at John, wishing she knew first aid. And then she saw his keys had fallen out of his pocket. She scooped them up and put them in the pocket in her skirt.

The ambulance men came in. They told everyone to stand clear. After what seemed to Agatha like an interminable wait he was carried out to the ambulance with a drip in his arm and an oxygen mask over his face.

The police arrived and took notes. 'Might be food poisoning, by the sound of it,' said one.

'Can I go home now?' asked the woman called Maggie. Her face was paper-white. 'I've had a terrible shock.'

'I suppose so,' said one. 'We'll just take a note of your names and addresses and then you can go. But you can't leave until then.'

There were exclamations of dismay from some of the other customers who, although they were half-way through perms and tints, just wanted to leave as quickly as possible. Maggie sat down and began to cry.

Agatha felt the keys burning a hole in her pocket. Why had she taken them?

Because, she thought, her brain sharpened by fear, perhaps he *was* a blackmailer, perhaps I've been as silly as Charles thinks I am. If he were a blackmailer, then he might have something on Mrs Friendly in his house. Poor Mrs Friendly. Why should she suffer more? Agatha did not realize that she had become a true villager: although Mrs Friendly was nothing more than an acquaintance, she felt she should be protected, even if it meant breaking the law.

She gave her name and address to one of the policemen. Her hair was still wet but she didn't care. She wanted to find out what was in that house and then somehow return with the keys and hide them somewhere in the salon. Besides, when Mr John recovered from his bout of food poisoning, which was what it had looked like, then she would know definitely one way or the other whether he was a villain or simply a very good hairdresser with nothing sinister about him to worry her. Her mind jumped to murder. Could it be murder? The police would not search his house because of simple food poisoning.

Oh yes, they would, she suddenly thought. They'll want to go through everything and find out what he ate. The Chinese meal! She hoped it wasn't that. But he would have developed symptoms of food poisoning before today and she herself would have fallen ill.

Feeling naked and exposed, she parked in

84

the back streets behind the Cheltenham Road and set off on foot for the villa. The neighbours might be watching and although they might not spot her, they might remember the make and registration number of any car parked outside the house. The day was so dark and still. As she cautiously approached the villa by way of the side street which ran along the side of it, she glanced nervously to right and left but no face glimmered at her through a window and no one was working in their garden.

After putting on a pair of gloves and fumbling with several of the keys, she found the right one and let herself in.

How many eyes had been watching her from the house opposite? She could say he had given her the keys before he collapsed. Oh, God, his staff would say he had done no such thing. But she was here and so she may as well get on with it.

She walked through the silent, dark, over-furnished rooms. No desk, no filing cabinet. She went upstairs. Two bedrooms showing no signs of recent occupation and then a large double bedroom, obviously his. She searched the bedside table and then the pockets of his jackets in the wardrobe.

Reluctant now to give up the search, she went slowly downstairs. And then, at the bottom of the stairs, she saw a door she had missed before. It was padlocked. A cellar door?

She tried all the keys until she had found the right one. Thunder rumbled in the distance.

She switched on the light inside the door and made her way down steep stone steps to a basement room. She was just reaching for the switch to illuminate the basement when she heard a noise above her head. She switched off the light on the stairs and stood in the darkness, panting like a hunted animal. The police must have arrived.

Agatha had a little torch in her handbag. If only she could find another way out of the basement! Her heart slowed down its pounding race. She cocked her head and listened hard. There were furtive noises from above. She frowned. The police would surely make more noise. Then a sinister gurgling sound. She had shut the door behind her at the top but the padlock was hanging open on the other side of the door.

Then there was a tremendous *whoosh* and she heard the upstairs street door close.

In one horrified split second she knew what had happened. Someone had set the house alight!

She switched on the basement light. A dusty room with exercise machines and weights and a desk in the corner—a desk that was under a dirty window.

Later Agatha was to reflect that a cool

detective would have seized papers from that desk, but all she could think of was the horror of burning to death.

She climbed on the desk and tugged at the window. It was firmly shut. She climbed down and heaved up one of the heaviest of the weights and hurled it at the window, which broke leaving a jagged hole. She smashed away the rest of the glass round the hole and with her gloved hands dragged herself up and through on to a patch of weedy earth outside.

She was in the garden at the side of the house, between the house and garage.

She crouched on her hands and knees behind a bush. How to get away unobserved? She took the keys from her pocket and threw them back in through the window.

Overhead came a great crack of thunder and the rain came down in sheets, so heavy it blotted out the view of the houses around.

A woman ran past down the street. Agatha had an excuse to be seen running hard.

She belted through the torrent, not stopping until she had reached her car.

Gasping and sobbing with fright, she drove off. She nearly ran into another car on the Four Pools Industrial Estate and realized she had not switched the windscreen wipers on.

She swung out on to the by-pass and made her way slowly and carefully home, through Broadway, up Fish Hill and along the escarpment past the Chipping Camden road, until she turned left and down through the tunnels of trees to Carsely.

She let herself into her cottage just as the rain began to slacken. She slammed the door shut behind her and slumped down on to the hall floor and took the phone on to her lap. She phoned Charles and said in a shaky voice, 'Come over. Something dreadful's happened.'

She found she was still wearing those gloves. She tore them off and carried them into the living-room. She put a whole packet of fire-lighters in the fireplace, then a bunch of kindling and lit the lot. When the flames were roaring up the chimney, she threw the gloves on to the fire. Her shoes! If there was anything left of the house, they would scan the carpets and find her footprints. She took off her shoes and threw them on the fire as well and then sat in front of the blaze, hugging herself and rocking to and fro.

When the doorbell rang, she gave a gulp of relief and went to open it. Charles stood there, as neat and immaculate as ever. She threw herself into his arms and began to cry.

'There now,' he said, shoving her inside. 'What have you been up to? What's that dreadful smell? Have you been burning old boots?'

He propelled her into the living-room. 'Sit down. I'll get us a brandy. You're all smoky and smelly and soaking wet.'

He poured two brandies and handed one to

Agatha. 'Now drink that and tell Uncle Charlie what happened. Did he rape you? No, you might have a smile on your face.'

'Don't be coarse. Are you one of those fools who think women *like* being raped?'

'Oh my God. You poor thing. It *was* rape. Look, Agatha. It's no longer the Dark Ages. We'll phone the police right now and—'

'IT WASN'T RAPE!' screamed Agatha.

'Well, what was it?'

'Sit down. Listen. I'll tell you. I can't believe I've been so stupid.'

Charles listened while Agatha told of the collapse of Mr John and how she had stolen his keys, about the house being set on fire.

'God, you're idiotic, Aggie,' he remarked. 'Someone's bound to have seen you. You might have got away with it if the house hadn't been torched. Police, forensics, experts from the insurance company, God, they'll be crawling over what's left inch by inch.'

'What am I to do?' wailed Agatha.

'Pray.'

'I mean, what am I really to do?'

'Well, if he was sick to the point of collapse and then someone torched his house, it looks to me as if someone tried to murder him. As they got him to the hospital, he'll probably be all right, and when he recovers he can maybe tell the police who he thinks did it.'

'Now it's you who is being stupid,' said Agatha. 'If he was a blackmailer, then he won't want to give the police the names of any suspects in case one of his victims tells all.'

'I know, we could pay him a visit, or rather you pay him a visit and tell him about taking his keys. Throw yourself on his mercy.'

'He might think I torched the house.'

'He probably knows who did it.'

'But what if he's not a blackmailer, but just an innocent philanderer?'

'I've a feeling he's a crook. But let's go to the hospital anyway.'

When they got to Evesham Hospital, it was to find that John had been transferred to the Mircester General Hospital.

'May as well go,' said Charles.

They drove in silence to Mircester.

'What's his second name?' asked Charles when he parked in front of the hospital.

'Shawpart.'

'Okay, here we go.'

They got out of the car.

'Oh, Aggie.'

'What?'

'How stupid we've been. You visited him twice, legitimately, so that will explain any fingerprint and footprints or loose hair. And how will they know they're your fingerprints anyway?'

'I got fingerprinted on one of the earlier cases.'

'Still, it's not too bad when you think about it. If they find the keys, they'll think the arsonist left them. Wait, that's odd.'

'What's odd?'

'You heard someone come in. You didn't hear anyone *break* in.'

Agatha stared at him in amazement. 'That's right.'

'So unless one of the neighbours saw you, you shouldn't be in any trouble at all. And if it's food poisoning, there won't be such a fuss. He's probably sitting up in bed, putting in his contact lenses.'

'I didn't know he wore contact lenses.'

'Aggie, those unnaturally blue eyes.'

'So that's why when I found him collapsed in the loo his eyes had gone grey?'

'Exactly.' He took her arm. 'I make a better detective than you any day.'

Chapter Four

They walked together into the hospital and up to the reception desk. 'We've called to visit John Shawpart,' said Charles.

She checked her records. 'He's in intensive care. Are you relatives?'

'I'm his sister,' said Agatha, and Charles groaned inwardly.

'If you go up to intensive care, someone will help you.'

'What the hell did you say that for?' hissed

Charles as they walked away.

'I can't leave here without knowing what's up with him.'

A nurse was sitting at a desk outside the intensive care unit.

'We've come to ask about Mr Shawpart,' said Agatha.

'Are you family?'

'His sister.'

'But surely the police told you . . . I am so sorry. Mr Shawpart died two hours ago.'

'What of?'

'Some sort of poisoning, but we will know definitely after the autopsy.'

'Thanks,' said Agatha, seizing hold of Charles's arm and turning to walk away.

'Wait a minute,' said the nurse sharply. 'I'll need your names.'

'In shock,' babbled Agatha and scurried off with Charles.

When they were outside, Charles said severely, 'You seem hell-bent on getting yourself into deeper water. The police will be given a description of you.'

'Never mind that. Someone must have poisoned him.'

'It could still be food poisoning. People do die of food poisoning. He might have had a dicky heart. We'll need to wait and see.'

'Let's drive past his house and see how much of it is left.'

'This is getting tiresome,' grumbled

Charles. 'Oh, very well.'

Agatha sat as he drove, her mind racing. She remembered James saying in Cyprus that she solved cases only by blundering about until the murderer betrayed himself, and that had hurt. Now it looked as if it were true. But it could not be murder, must not be murder.

When they reached the Cheltenham Road in Evesham and approached the house, they could see the police tape that cordoned off the blackened shell. They slowed down as they went past. A policeman on duty stared at the car suspiciously and Charles sped off.

'There wasn't much of that left,' he said. 'That noise you heard, that gurgling sound, must have been petrol.'

'Looks like it,' said Agatha wearily.

'Cheer up. There won't be much trace of anything left.'

'Including who he was blackmailing, if he was blackmailing.'

'All we can do is wait and see.'

*   *   *

Agatha waited all the next day but no policeman came. By the end of the second day, she was beginning to relax, beginning to think it might have been a simple case of food poisoning, when a ring at the doorbell made her jump.

She opened the door. Detective Sergeant

Bill Wong stood there, his round face stern. He was flanked by a policewoman. 'Mind if we come in, Mrs Raisin?'

Mrs Raisin. Not Agatha.

Agatha stepped back and let them in. 'How nice to see you, Bill,' she chattered. 'I'll just make us some coffee.'

'No coffee. This is business.'

She led them into the living-room. They sat down on a sofa, side by side. Agatha quickly put a fire-guard in front of the blackened mess in the grate, which she had forgotten to clear out.

She sat down nervously on a chair facing them.

'You knew Mr John Shawpart?' began Bill.

'Yes, he was my hairdresser.'

'Anything closer?'

'Yes, we were friends. We had a couple of meals.'

His eyes were hard. 'Let's begin at the beginning. I see from the list of customers that you were present when he fell sick.'

'Yes.'

'And a woman answering to your description called at the intensive ward at Mircester Hospital, claiming to be his sister.'

Agatha briefly considered lying and then decided against it.

'Well, yes. I wanted to find out what had happened. Why are you handling this case, Bill? Surely Worcester CID is in charge.'

'They've asked for our help, and as you live in Gloucestershire, I have the job of interviewing you. You could be in bad trouble for claiming to be a family member.'

'What is this?' demanded Agatha, her face becoming flushed with anger. 'What happened to him? I thought it was food poisoning.'

'Ricin.'

'What's that?'

'It's a poison made from castor-oil beans. John Shawpart was murdered. And if we hadn't got a damned clever pathologist who had made a study of ricin poisoning, we'd still be looking. So settle down and tell us everything you know.'

Agatha decided to tell most of the truth but to omit that she had been in his house when it was set on fire.

'It's like this,' she said. 'I heard a rumour that he was a blackmailer and decided to get to know him better and find out.'

'And what made you think he was a blackmailer?'

'Just a feeling. Women talked a lot to him at the salon about their private lives and I saw him with a couple of women and they both looked distressed and frightened.'

'Names?'

Agatha thought furiously. She could not betray Mrs Friendly after having gone to such lengths to try to protect her.

'I recognized one of them from the salon. I

95

think her first name is Maggie. It's all first names there.'

'Description?'

'Well, brown hair, sort of ordinary, rather protuberant eyes. She was there the first time I went. She was complaining that her husband didn't understand her or something and then I went for a trip on the river with a friend and I saw her sitting in that tea garden before the bridge with John and she looked unhappy.'

'This still does not explain why you thought he was a blackmailer, or, if you thought he was, why then you were prepared to go into business with him.'

Agatha turned red. 'How did you hear that?'

'He told his assistant Garry about it.'

'I was stringing him along. I wanted to see if he would betray himself.'

'This still does not explain why you leaped to the conclusion he was a blackmailer.'

'It was just an intuition,' said Agatha desperately. 'Look, I was having dinner with him one night in a restaurant, and when we were leaving, this woman was staring at him and her face was a mask of fear.'

'What woman?'

'I didn't recognize her,' lied Agatha.

'Description.'

'A small sort of weasel woman, black hair, glasses,' said Agatha desperately.

'Hum. And who was this male friend who

accompanied you to the hospital?'

'Charles, Sir Charles Fraith.'

Bill took out a mobile phone. 'Phone number?'

'I can't remember offhand.'

'Then go and get me the phone book.'

Agatha wanted to speak to Charles before Bill got to him.

She went into the hall and picked up the phone book. The door was standing open. She threw the phone book out over the hedge.

She went back in. 'Can't find it.'

He gave her a cynical look, dialled directory inquiries, got Charles's number, dialled it while Agatha prayed that Charles would not be at home. But with a sinking heart she heard Bill say, 'Sir Charles, we are with Mrs Raisin. I wonder whether you could join us. There are some questions we would like to ask you. Good. See you soon.'

There was a scrabbling of paws and Mrs Darry entered the room. In one hand she clutched a phone book. 'Really, Mrs Raisin,' she said, 'if you want rid of your phone book, you should put it in the bin.'

'I don't know what you are talking about,' said Agatha.

'You nearly hit my little poochie with it. You threw it over your hedge.'

Agatha snatched the phone book from her. 'Would you mind leaving? I'm busy.'

Mrs Darry's eyes gleamed with curiosity.

Bill rose and said, 'Yes, this is private business, so if you don't mind . . .'

Mrs Darry left, her thin shoulders seeming to radiate frustrated curiosity.

'So let's go back to the day John Shawpart was murdered,' said Bill. 'Tell us about it.'

Relieved for the moment to get away from the blackmailing question, Agatha described how he had looked ill, had gone to the toilet, how she and everyone else in the salon had heard the terrible retching, how she had got the tool-box and broken the lock of the toilet door and had found the hairdresser collapsed on the floor.

'I thought it was food poisoning,' she said. 'How could I think anything else? We had eaten a Chinese meal at his house the evening before . . .'

'So you were with him the evening before he died. Do you know how he got the bruising on his face?'

'Oh, that. I was at his house before that. I was told at the salon that he was ill and I found his address and went there. I was shocked at the state of his face. He said he'd been in a car accident but hadn't bothered to report it. He said he hadn't been wearing his seat-belt and had hit the windscreen, but when I left I noticed his car was at the side of the house and that it was unmarked, so I thought maybe some jealous husband might have socked him.'

'And why should you think that?'

'Well, it was seeing him with that customer, Maggie, and then he did come on to me. I supposed he made a habit of chatting up women.'

'Do you know his house was set on fire on the day of the murder?'

'Yes, someone told me,' lied Agatha. 'I forget who.'

'It was arson. Someone poured petrol over the place and set it alight.'

'Was anyone seen?'

'The people in the surrounding villas all unfortunately work and the few exceptions that don't were not looking.'

Agatha stifled the sigh of relief that had risen to her lips.

He looked at her directly. 'Did you have anything to do with that or know anything about it?'

So many lies, thought Agatha wearily. 'No,' she said.

'We'll leave that for the moment. Go over what happened at the salon again.'

Agatha described again in detail what had happened. Then she heard a car drawing up outside. Charles! What on earth was he going to say?

Charles breezed it. 'Hello, Bill. What's this? The third degree?'

'Sit down, Sir Charles.'

'Formal, hey? Okay, it must be about that

damned hairdresser. Murdered, was he?'

'Yes.'

'How?'

'Ricin poisoning.'

'Ricin? Pretty exotic. That's the stuff that killed that Bulgarian defector when he was working with the BBC in London in the seventies. Markov. That was his name. Stuff of spy fiction, Aggie. He got stabbed in the leg with an umbrella and the ricin was injected into him that way. They found a metal pellet had been injected into his leg. Hey, I remember them saying that ricin is almost impossible to detect and has no antidote. So how did they get on to it?'

'The pathologist, by coincidence, had been fascinated with the Markov case and had read all the medical notes on it. The tiny platinum sphere, just 1.77 millimetres in diameter and drilled through with two tiny 0.35 millimetre holes to carry the ricin, is now in the Black Museum at Scotland Yard.'

'Was the same thing done to this hairdresser?'

'No, he appears to have swallowed the ricin. There were traces of gelatin. We believe it might have been put into pills of some sort.'

'Lifex,' said Agatha suddenly.

'What's that?' demanded Bill.

'Vitamin pills. He showed me a bottle of them. Said they were multi-vitamins and that he kept a bottle in the salon as well. They were large and gelatin-covered.'

'Now we're getting somewhere,' said Bill eagerly. 'I'll just phone that through.'

He went into the hall with his mobile phone. Agatha longed to warn Charles not to say too much, but the policewoman, a large and stolid female, sat studying them closely as if they were both some rare species of animal.

Bill came back and sat down.

'In view of your knowledge, Detective Inspector John Brudge of Worcester CID will be over to see you as well.'

Agatha groaned. 'I've told you everything I know.'

Bill ignored her and turned his attention to Charles.

'Now, Sir Charles, where do you come into this? Were you under the impression that John Shawpart was a blackmailer?'

'I got that idea first from Aggie here. I decided it would be fun to find out and egged her on. I persuaded her to go out with him for dinner and tell him that James Lacey was coming back and she was terrified he would find out about us and so she was to tape the whole thing and see if he demanded money for her silence, but it all went wrong.'

'What happened?'

'To reinforce Aggie's fiction, I turned up here to wait until they arrived back from the restaurant to play the part of the jealous lover. Unfortunately I did it a bit too well. I grabbed

101

Aggie's arm and her handbag went spinning and the tape recorder fell out and he saw it.'

'Did he say anything?'

'Let me see, he said something like, "Yours, I think." He looked amused in a nasty way, but as I explained to Aggie afterwards, lots of people carry these little machines around with them.'

'But he asked Mrs Raisin to go into business with him, so he cannot think you suspected him of anything.'

'Well,' said Agatha reluctantly, 'that was because I managed to make him think I had fallen for him.'

Bill leaned back in his chair. 'I must ask you again: what made both of you persist in thinking he was a blackmailer?'

'I told Bill we saw that ferrety-looking woman, I mean John and me, when we left a restaurant, and she looked so white and frightened,' said Agatha, trying to signal with her eyes to Charles not to betray Mrs Friendly.

'Oh, I can tell you all about that,' said Charles breezily. Agatha groaned inwardly.

'We were bored,' said Charles.

'I beg your pardon?' exclaimed Bill.

'Bored. Ennui. Fed up. No interest. So when Aggie said teasingly that she was sure he was a blackmailer, I went along with it, worked her up, you know. All a bit of fun.'

'And now he's dead, murdered,' said Bill

evenly.

'And so he is, which shows he must have been up to some malarkey after all and it's up to you to find out what it was. But we had nothing to do with it.'

'You went to the hospital, Sir Charles, with Mrs Raisin here. She said she was the deceased's sister. Then, despite the fact that Mrs Raisin told us before you arrived that someone had told her that Shawpart's house had been burnt, your car was spotted driving slowly past on the night of the murder.'

'I was curious to see where he lived,' said Charles blandly.

'All right, let's go back over some points. Which restaurant were you in, Mrs Raisin, when you saw this frightened woman?'

'The bistro that's attached to the Crown Inn in Blockley.'

'You said that the night before he died you shared a Chinese meal with him. Which restaurant?'

'He sent out for it. I can't remember which one.'

'This business he meant to start in London. According to that assistant Garry, John Shawpart seemed under the impression that you were so besotted with him that you were prepared to pay for the whole thing.'

Agatha turned dark red with mortification.

'Good act you put on, Aggie,' said Charles. 'He must have believed you were really

103

smitten.'

'Ah, yes, you said it was an act,' said Bill. 'That will be all for the moment. You will both be expected to make statements.'

'When will Worcester CID be calling?' asked Agatha.

'Quite soon.'

'Then I'd better stay,' said Charles cheerfully, 'and let them deal with both of us at once.'

Agatha stood up to show Bill and the policewoman out, her legs stiff with tension.

'We'll be in touch, Mrs Raisin,' said Bill, avoiding the hurt and rejected look in Agatha's eyes.

She nodded to him, shut the door on them both, joined Charles in the living-room and burst into tears.

*   *   *

Bill got into the police car and took the wheel. The policewoman got in on the passenger side. The reason that Bill had been so cold and formal with Agatha was that he was accompanied by Snoopy Christine, the bane of Mircester police headquarters. She delighted in finding out weaknesses in her fellow officers and gossiping about them to anyone who would listen.

Her first words when they had set out from Mircester earlier had been, 'Rumour has it that you're a friend of this Agatha Raisin's.'

And Bill, who knew Agatha was in trouble over pretending to be the dead man's sister and was well aware that any sign of warmth towards Agatha on his part would be reported by the beady-eyed Christine, had said casually, 'Just some woman I met on some cases.'

'Her husband was murdered, wasn't he?'

'Yes, I was on that case.'

On the road back after interviewing Agatha and Charles, Christine said nastily, 'They're nothing more than a couple of rich layabouts, amusing themselves by playing at detectives.'

'Exactly,' said Bill casually. With any luck, all Agatha would get would be a rap over the knuckles for having pretended to be Shawpart's sister. Any sign of favouritism on his part, and Christine would put it about and it might get to Worcester and they might feel compelled to punish Agatha to show that the police did not have favourites.

* * *

'Come on now, Aggie,' Charles was saying in a soothing voice, 'it looks as if you're off the hook. No one saw you going to his house after he was murdered.'

Agatha dried her eyes and blew her nose. 'It's Bill,' she said. 'He was my very first friend and now he's gone off me.'

She cleaned the burnt mess out of the

fireplace, put it in a garbage bag, ran out and slung the bag into James's garden. She returned to Charles.

'Probably had to be formal in front of that cow of a policewoman. Brace yourself. I think the heavy mob's arrived.'

*   *   *

Detective Inspector John Brudge was an intelligent-looking man with dark hair and a thin, clever face. He brought not only a detective sergeant and a detective constable with him, but two uniformed officers and a search warrant.

While he took Agatha and Charles carefully through their stories again, Agatha could hear the forces of law and order moving through the cottage, searching every drawer, cupboard and nook and cranny.

It was annoying rather than worrying, for she had nothing to hide. She had even wiped her conversation with the hairdresser from her tape recorder.

The one main thing that was making her begin to relax was that no one had seen her at the villa on the Cheltenham Road on the day it was burnt down.

Just as the long interrogation was coming to an end, the detective constable entered and quietly handed Brudge a receipt. Agatha stiffened and looked wildly at Charles. It was an Asprey's receipt for those cuff-links. Then she began to relax again. She could say she had bought them for Charles and Charles would be quick enough, she was sure, to agree.

Brudge moved out into the hall with the receipt. She then heard him talking into his phone but could not make out the words.

He came back in holding the receipt and sat down.

'This is a receipt for a pair of very expensive cuff-links, Mrs Raisin, gold cuff-links.'

'Yes,' said Agatha easily. 'I bought them as a present for Charles here.'

He looked at her steadily for a few moments and then he said, 'In the part of the living-room of Shawpart's house which survived, we found a box containing a pair of gold cuff-links from Asprey's. I think you bought them for Shawpart, Mrs Raisin, and it is no use denying it because we can easily check.'

'I bought those for Charles,' protested Agatha.

'Who can no doubt produce them?'

'It's no use, Aggie,' said Charles. 'Why lie when we have no reason to? I urged her to buy Shawpart some expensive present to get close to him.'

'Why?'

'I told you. It was a game. We were sure he

107

was up to something fishy.'

'An expensive game. You have both gone on about finding out about this hairdresser for fun, because you were bored. I find that hard to believe. You initially lied, Mrs Raisin, although Sir Charles here says you have nothing to hide. I find that very suspicious. You will call at Mircester tomorrow and sign your statements. You are not to travel abroad until this investigation is completed.'

'I'm sorry I lied,' said Agatha, 'but I feel embarrassed about wasting so much money on him. And I wasn't to know he would be murdered.'

'So you say. I have yet to read the Gloucester report. I hope you have not been lying to them as well.'

Agatha thought about her saying that someone had told her the villa had burnt down and then finding out Charles's car had been spotted. She groaned inwardly.

'We are taking some things,' said Brudge. A policeman held out a box containing a few bottles of vitamin pills and aspirin. 'We will give you a receipt for them.'

When they had all left, she said to Charles, 'What a mess.'

'Are you hungry?'

'Not very.'

'Let's go along to the Red Lion and get a sandwich.'

'All right. Give me a moment while I

change. I feel all sweaty.'

She went up to her bathroom and stripped and had a quick shower and put on a clean blouse and skirt.

She looked out of the window. Charles was playing with her cats in the garden. He had made a ball out of kitchen foil and was throwing it in the air while the cats leaped up to catch it.

Did he ever worry about anything? Probably just as well if he did not. She herself was worrying enough for the whole of the Cotswolds.

The lounge bar of the Red Lion was smoky and dim. A fire had been lit and little puffs of grey smoke escaped from it and lay in bands across the low-beamed room.

They collected gin and tonics and ham sandwiches and retreated to a far corner.

'So what do we do now?' asked Agatha.

'We go on. For a start we've got to try to get the Friendly woman on her own.'

'How do we do that?'

'You're all kerfuffled and discombobulated these days, Aggie. You put me up for the night and then we watch her house and see if Mr Friendly leaves.'

'How can we do that without being too obvious?'

'The cottage is opposite the churchyard. You take me on a tour of the graves. I'm a historian. I make notes. Even if he doesn't leave, surely she goes out shopping. Then we should get to a library and read up on ricin. Are there any castor-oil plants outside Kew Gardens in this country, for example? If not, which of our suspects has been abroad lately?'

'I don't think we've really got any suspects.'

'Wake up! Of course we have. We have the hairy Mr Friendly. We have the woman Maggie. We'll start with them.'

'We can't haunt the Friendlys tomorrow morning. We've got to go to Mircester.'

'So we have. After, then.'

'I'm still hurt by Bill's behaviour,' fretted Agatha. 'Badly hurt. First, he's on holiday and doesn't phone, then he's on duty and treats me like Suspect Number One.'

'Why don't you just phone him? You've got his phone number.'

'I don't want to,' mumbled Agatha.

'You're frightened he's gone off you because of some deep unlikeable flaw in your character, so you prefer to be miserable. Tell you what, I'll go home and pack a bag. I'll be staying with you.'

Agatha raised a smile. 'No funny stuff.'

'Did I ever? See you back at the ranch, Aggie.'

He went off. She finished her drink, but instead of going home, walked to the vicarage and rang the bell.

'Christ!' came the unholy voice of the vicar. 'It's that woman again.'

'Don't blaspheme, Alf, and get on with your sermon,' came Mrs Bloxby's calm voice.

'I always call at the wrong time,' said Agatha ruefully as Mrs Bloxby opened the door.

'Pay no attention to Alf. He's the same with everyone. I keep telling him he's too antisocial for a vicar. Come in.'

'If you're sure . . .'

'Quite sure. Tea? Coffee?'

'A cup of coffee would be nice.'

'Come into the kitchen.'

The kitchen was warm and welcoming. Bunches of dried herbs hung from the ceiling and shining copper pans gleamed against the old stone walls. 'I've got some ready,' said Mrs Bloxby, pouring two mugs.

Agatha said, 'Can we take this into the garden? Then I can smoke with a free conscience.'

'Certainly, although I hope you don't find it too chilly. It's got quite cold since the weather broke.

'Now,' said Mrs Bloxby when they were both seated, 'I know the police were at your cottage and all because of that hairdresser. I wish I had never recommended him. Is it murder?'

Agatha described all the things she had done and left undone. A large barn owl, ghostly in the dark, swooped over their heads, and sleepy birds chirped lazily in the surrounding trees.

'I've been so very stupid,' commented Agatha when she had finished her tale.

'I think all the effort you went to on Mrs Friendly's behalf,' said Mrs Bloxby, 'shows a noble spirit. Perhaps you should tell her. She must be dreadfully frightened that the police may have found something.'

'So you do think she could have been a victim of blackmail!'

'Just an idea.'

'Does Mr Friendly go out? I mean, is she ever on her own?'

'He plays golf practically every afternoon between two and five.'

'Thank you,' said Agatha. 'I don't feel so silly now.'

'In the meantime, I shall ask around about a woman called Maggie and give your description. The joy about being a vicar's wife is that I can ask questions about people and no one thinks it suspicious.'

'I'd better go. Charles will be back any minute. He's staying the night. I mean, you know, I don't mean . . .'

Mrs Bloxby laughed. 'Off you go. And phone Bill Wong. There's bound to be a simple explanation.'

*   *   *

'So what's happened to you?' demanded

Charles as she let him in. 'All calm and smiling now. Been at the Prozac?'

'Been seeing Mrs Bloxby.'

'Ah, confession is good for the soul.'

Agatha led him up to the spare bedroom.

'While you're putting your things away, I'll make a phone call.'

She went down to the kitchen extension and dialled Bill Wong's home number.

She prayed his formidable mother would not answer the phone and it was with relief that she recognized Bill's voice. 'Bill, it's Agatha.'

'Oh.'

'Bill, what happened? You were on holiday and you didn't phone.'

His voice to her relief sounded amused. 'The phone works both ways, Agatha.'

'I thought you'd gone away on holiday until Charles said he saw you in Mircester.'

'A heavy romance, Agatha.'

'And what was all the formality today about? You treated me like a criminal.'

'Just as well, too. I was accompanied by Snoopy Christine and you've got me in deep shit already, Agatha.'

'Why?'

'I did not put in my report that you had lied about driving past the villa with Charles. I don't know why you did that.'

'I was confused.'

'Anyway, Snoopy Christine somehow got

113

hold of my report and felt duty-bound to point out the omission to Detective Inspector Wilkes, who gave me a lecture on the dangers of favouritism. Then you tried to pretend you hadn't Charles's number and threw that phone book over the hedge. I'd left that bit out as well. Christine pointed out that omission too.'

'Oh, gosh, I'm sorry, but I felt guilty because of your coldness and about us playing amateur detectives.'

'I know you well, Agatha, and when you said you knew nothing about the fire, I could swear you were lying.'

'Well, I wasn't,' said Agatha hotly. She knew that if she confessed to Bill that she had actually been inside when the house went on fire, then he would have to report her and she would probably be arrested for arson, along with impeding the police in their inquiries and anything else they could throw at her.

'Keep in touch with me and let me know if you think of anything you might have missed out,' said Bill. 'But it's mostly Worcester's case. Don't flap about and get yourself nearly killed like you've been doing in the past. And remember that Worcester CID are very clever.'

'There are cases you would never have solved if it hadn't been for me,' said Agatha huffily.

'I've told you and told you, the police

always get there sooner or later. Take a break. Relax. Get a hobby.'

'You're patronizing.'

'I'm cross because I got into trouble trying to cover up for you.'

'Sorry.'

'We'll meet soon, Agatha.'

'Okay, how's the romance?'

'Dead in the water. I don't know what happened.'

'Take her home to meet the parents and all that?' asked Agatha with affected casualness.

'Yes, but it still collapsed.'

Poor Bill, thought Agatha. Mr and Mr Wong were enough to scare off any girl. But he adored his parents and she knew that any criticism of them would wound him deeply.

'Isn't ricin an odd sort of poison?'

'Not all that odd. The murderer could have got away with it. It's terribly hard to detect, almost impossible.'

'Seems to point to a pretty sophisticated murderer,' said Agatha. 'I mean, it's not the sort of thing some ordinary village housewife would use.'

'Why did you say that?' His voice was sharp. 'What ordinary village housewife did you have in mind?'

'I didn't. I mean I just meant that it was a very exotic sort of poison.'

'If you say so.' Suspicious. 'I feel there's a lot you're holding back.'

115

Agatha managed a light laugh. 'Don't I tell you everything?'

'Not always, no.'

'We'll have a drink and a meal soon, Bill.'

'Right. Go carefully. See you.'

Agatha replaced the receiver. Instead of being relieved to find they were still friends, she now felt worried and guilty about lying to Bill.

*   *   *

They made their statements the following day at Mircester police headquarters and emerged from a gruelling session blinking in the mellow sunlight. Good weather had returned, but without the ferocious heat, and there was an autumnal crispness in the air.

'It's still morning,' said Charles, 'and at least you're still free. Haven't bagged you up yet, which is a miracle. So what do we do now? Confront Mrs Friendly?'

'Bit early. The hairy husband doesn't play golf until the afternoon.'

'So let's try the library and read up on castor-oil plants.'

Mircester Public Library was dark and silent, a marble-pillared, cavernous Victorian place. Agatha's high heels clicked across the marble floor.

'Where do we start?' she whispered.

'We'll look up an encyclopedia.'

116

They searched along the reference shelves. 'Here we are,' said Charles. '*R* for ricin.'

He flicked the pages. 'Nothing here.'

'Try *P* for poison,' suggested Agatha.

'Right you are. Now let me see. Ah, poisonous plants. Here we go. Listen to this, Agatha.

' "Castor-oil plant. *Ricinus communis*. Large plant of the spurge family grown commercially for the pharmaceutical and industrial uses of oil and for use in landscaping because of its handsome, giant, twelve-lobed palmate (fanlike) leaves. The brittle spinel, bronze-to-red clusters of fruits are attractive but often removed before they mature because of the poison, ricinine, concentrated in their mottled bean-like seeds. Probably native to Africa—" '

'Not Evesham, then. Rats,' interrupted Agatha.

'Listen and learn,' he said severely. ' "Probably native to Africa, this species has become naturalized throughout the tropical world. The plants are cultivated chiefly in India and Brazil, largely for their oil." Aha, here we go! "In temperate climates they are raised as annuals and grow onc point five to two point four feet in a single season." There! This is a temperate climate. Ergo, all we need to do is keep looking in gardens.'

He flicked over another page. 'Here are the symptoms of ricin poisoning. "Burning of mouth, throat and stomach, vomiting, diarrhoea, abdominal cramps, dulled vision, respiratory distress, paralysis, death."'

Agatha repressed a shudder. 'What a way to go! Let's go and eat and see if we can catch Mrs Friendly on her own.'

*   *   *

At two o'clock that afternoon, they left the car outside Agatha's cottage and walked towards the church. 'We'll wander amongst the gravestones,' said Charles. 'I'll look knowledgeable and take notes and you yack away as if you're telling me the history. Look at this tombstone. Five children, died so young, and they talk about the good old days. Why do people keep talking about the good old days, Aggie?'

'Nostalgia. If people have had a reasonable childhood, then they remember a time when the days always seemed to be sunny and they had no responsibilities, like work or paying the bills, and grown-ups were some sort of know-all superior giants. Funny, that. It even works for me with the recent past. When I'm depressed and things aren't moving forward, my mind harks back to the London days and what a marvellous time I had, when, come to think of it, I didn't really have a marvellous time.' Agatha frowned in thought. 'I suppose no matter how old one is, one has to always

118

have a goal. Study something. What?'

Charles had muttered a soft exclamation. 'I got a glimpse of Mr Friendly driving off.'

'We'll give it a few minutes,' said Agatha. 'You know, I'm a bit apprehensive about all this. Why not leave it to the police?'

'Solving this murder is your goal, Aggie. We'll ask a few questions here and there, see how we get on, and when it becomes tiresome, we'll jack it in.'

'This is just a game for you!'

Charles shrugged. 'Why not? Take all this murder and mayhem too seriously and you'll go barmy. Let's go and see Mrs Friendly.'

*   *   *

Liza Friendly looked as if she did not want to let them in. 'Just a few moments of your time,' pleaded Agatha.

'Very well, but I've got a lot to do.'

They sat down in the small, dark living room. Liza did not offer them tea or coffee but sat facing them, perched on the edge of a chair, her hands clasped in her lap.

Agatha decided to get straight to the point. 'That hairdresser, Mr John of Evesham, was killed . . . murdered.'

'It was food poisoning!' Mrs Friendly's eyes darted this way and that as if looking for escape.

'It's in the papers this morning,' said

Agatha. She and Charles had bought the newspapers on the way back from Mircester.

Her hands twisted nervously in her lap. 'I don't read the newspapers.'

But Agatha noted she did not wonder why they were questioning her.

'You knew Mr John.' Agatha made it a statement, rather than a question.

'Well, I went to his salon a few times. But then it seemed an unnecessary expense. I do my hair myself now.'

And it looks it, thought Agatha brutally.

She took a deep breath. 'So when did he start blackmailing you?'

Liza leapt to her feet. 'Get out of here!' she shouted. 'Get out of my house.'

'Sit down,' said Charles quietly. 'We haven't told the police, and Aggie here went to great lengths to destroy the evidence.'

Liza sat down suddenly, as if her legs had given way. She said through dry lips, 'If my husband finds out, he'll kill me.'

'I'll be in more of a fix with the police than you if they find out what I did.' Agatha told her about going to the hairdresser's home to try to get hold of anything that might incriminate Mrs Friendly.

'So you see,' she ended, 'it's in your interest to help us. We must find out who really did it.'

There was a long silence. Oh, hurry up, thought Agatha. What if that husband of yours has left something behind and comes

120

back for it?

Then Liza said with a sigh, 'I was fascinated by him. He made me feel attractive. We began to meet occasionally for a coffee, and then, a few months ago, Bob went off to Scotland to play golf with an old school friend. We went out for dinner and then we went back to his house.'

She fell silent. 'You slept with him,' prompted Agatha.

'Yes.'

'So then what happened?'

'He'd found out I had some money of my own. My mother left me some in her will that was in a separate bank account under my name. After that one night, he didn't call, didn't get in touch. I went to the salon several times, but he always got someone else to do my hair. I was frantic. I loved him. I thought I could leave Bob and go away with him. I wrote him several letters, pleading with him, reminding him of our love. And then he phoned and arranged to meet me in the salon after hours. He produced those letters and said unless I paid him, he would send the letters to my husband. Bob has a frightful temper. John wanted five thousand pounds. He said that would be enough and he would let me have the letters. So I paid him.'

Agatha looked at her with pity. 'But you didn't get the letters. He asked for more.'

Liza nodded.

'Did you give it to him?'

'I told him to wait, I needed time. Then I heard he was dead and I felt I had escaped from hell.'

Agatha looked around the poky cottage. 'If you have money of your own and I assume your husband has money, why do you live in such a small place?'

'Bob always says we should keep hold of a lot of money for our old age. Old folks' homes cost so much.'

'If your husband is as tyrannical as you make out, it's a wonder he didn't insist your money went into a joint account.'

'We never had one. Before Mother died, he gave me a weekly allowance. When I got my own money, he said I could use that.'

'You didn't give John Shawpart a cheque, did you?' asked Charles.

She shook her head. 'No, he wanted cash. I paid him in cash.'

'Good, the police won't find any record of the payment in his bank.' Charles leaned forward. 'You don't think your husband could have found out anything? Shawpart was beaten up just before his death.'

'Oh, no. Bob would never have kept such a thing to himself.'

'Have you any children?' asked Agatha.

She shook her head sadly. 'We were never able to have any. I wanted to adopt, but Bob said the kid could turn out to be a psychopath and he wouldn't hear of it.'

'Didn't you ever work?' asked Agatha.

'I was a secretary when I met Bob. Shorthand and typing. I sometimes thought of going back to work, but Bob said nobody would want me. It's all computers now.'

'Computing can be learned,' said Agatha.

'Bob would never let me.'

'Look, you've got your own money. Have you a car? Can you drive?'

'Yes, I have a little car.'

'So why don't you just get in the car one day when he's out and drive off,' said Agatha. 'Start a new life somewhere else.'

'Oh, I couldn't!'

'Why?'

'What would Bob do without me? Who would cook his meals and iron his shirts?'

'He would just have to learn to do that himself,' said Agatha, exasperated.

'We're getting away from the point,' said Charles hurriedly. 'Now, think. Did you ever see John Shawpart with any other women?'

Liza sat silently for a moment, a faint blush rising to her cheeks. Then she said, 'When he had stopped getting in touch with me after . . . after that night, I would drive to his house, on Sundays and half day, Wednesday, and watch. I was mad with jealousy. There was one woman paid him a visit—Maggie, I think her name is. I've seen her in the salon. Then another time, I saw Mrs Darry coming out of his house.'

Agatha stared at her. '*Our* Mrs Darry? The terror of Carsely?'

'Yes, her. But she was probably collecting for something.'

'Well, well. Anyone else?'

'A young pretty woman, thirties, that's young to me. I hadn't seen her before.'

'What did she look like?'

'Blonde, slim, a bit rabbity, rather prominent teeth, skinny legs.'

'Anyone else?'

'No. It's God's punishment on me!'

'I don't think God punishes or rewards,' said Charles unexpectedly. 'Those are both such human failings, starting off with, "If you're good, Santa will give you a bike for Christmas." I never got one because I was told that Santa was mad at me for blocking up the chimney and smoking out the house.'

Agatha blinked at him in surprise and then went on, 'Liza—may I call you Liza?'

She nodded.

'The thing is, Liza, don't worry about the police. Do you think anyone might have seen you with Mr John?'

'I don't think so. Perhaps his neighbours . . .'

'But his neighbours didn't know you?'

'No.'

'So at the worst, all they can give is a description, and you'll probably be lost in all the other descriptions of women Mr John was seen with.'

'How was he poisoned?'

'Ricin.'

'What's that?'

'It's a poison from castor-oil beans.'

'But I've never even heard of it!'

There was the sound of a key in the door. Agatha glanced out of the cottage window and noticed the leaded panes were smeared with rain.

'Bob!' said Liza.

'So that's all settled,' said Agatha. She raised her voice. 'You're like me, Mrs Friendly, and don't want to perform at any of their concerts, but I would appreciate your help with the catering on the next occasion. Why, Mr Friendly! We were just leaving.'

'Good,' he said rudely, swinging a bag of golf clubs from his shoulder and stacking them in a corner. 'Bloody rain.'

Agatha and Charles got up and made their way to the door. 'My wife has enough to do with the housekeeping here without wasting time on parish affairs,' he said as they edged past him.

'Quite,' murmured Agatha. 'Such a pleasure to meet you again.'

'Tcha!'

'And ya sucks boo to you too,' said Agatha when she and Charles emerged into the pouring rain. 'Let's run. I'm getting soaked.'

They ran all the way to Agatha's cottage. They dried themselves off in their respective rooms, changed into dry clothes and met up again in the kitchen.

'Well,' said Agatha, 'what did you make of that? Mrs Darry!'

'Who's she?'

'The ferrety woman with the nasty little dog.'

'Ah, the one who retrieved your phone book.'

'The same.'

'So do we tackle her next?'

'I suppose so, although she's going to be most dreadfully rude. Damn, if it hadn't been for Liza, I would be regretting having tried to rescue any incriminating papers. God, would I love to have some dirt on Mrs Darry.'

'What's her first name?'

'In the ladies' society of Carsely, Charles, first names do not exist. We are all Miss this and Mrs that.'

'Where does she live?'

'Grim little house called Parks Cottage up Parks Lane, at the back of the village shop.'

'The rain is easing off. I think we should go before you lose courage. Maybe she'll have a garden full of castor-oil plants.'

Agatha hesitated. 'What sort of approach are we going to take?'

'Nasty and blunt, I should think, dear Aggie. Sort of thing you do best.'

Chapter Five

Watery sunlight struck down on the cobbles as they made their way to Mrs Darry's cottage. Not for one moment would Agatha admit to herself that she was intimidated by the waspish Mrs Darry and yet she experienced a sinking feeling as they approached the cottage and she saw that the door was standing open and the nasty little dog was snuffling about the steps.

'No castor-oil plants,' commented Charles, looking around the small front garden. 'Nothing but laurels and other dreary shrubs. Wonder what's round the back.'

Mrs Darry appeared at her front door. Her greeting was typical. 'What do you want?'

'We wanted to have a word with you.' Agatha surreptitiously edged the snuffling dog away from her ankles with her foot.

'I don't think I should invite you in,' said Mrs Darry, her thin face bright with malice. 'I have my reputation to think of.'

'What's that supposed to mean?' Agatha, irritated, gave the little dog another kick.

'I don't think I should let you and one of your fancy men into my home.'

Charles brayed with laughter and Agatha glared at Mrs Darry.

'Okay,' she said truculently, raising her

voice. 'We'll stand out here and discuss *your* fancy man, the late Mr John Shawpart.'

For once, Agatha had obviously scored over the terrible Mrs Darry, whose green eyes goggled and then darted right and left. 'Come in,' she said abruptly. Her little dog raised his leg and peed on to Agatha's shoe.

'Oh, for Christ's sake!' howled Agatha. The dog scampered into the house. Agatha removed her shoe and, taking out a tissue, wiped it clean.

'Supposed to be lucky, Aggie,' said Charles. 'Let's go in before she changes her mind and slams the door on us.'

Another dark cottage living-room, everything in shades of dull green: green velvet upholstered three-piece suite, green walls, dark green fitted carpet, green leaves from the thick ivy outside which covered the cottage, blocking out any light the small windows might have afforded. All sat down and faced each other in this subterranean gloom.

'What did you mean by that remark?' demanded Mrs Darry. The dog leapt on her lap and she kneaded her thin fingers in its coat.

'John Shawpart was a blackmailer,' said Agatha. 'He wooed women, found out about them, and then blackmailed them.'

'Rubbish!' Mrs Darry sounded breathless. 'I'm a respectable woman. Who could possibly want to blackmail me? I am not like you, Mrs Raisin, with your scandalous affairs with younger men.'

Checkmate, thought Agatha. What could there be in this acidulous woman's life that was worth a blackmailer's time?

'Money,' said Charles suddenly. 'It was all about money. We know that.'

He was half talking to himself, but Mrs Darry stared at him like a rat hypnotized by a snake.

'You know,' she said through dry lips.

Agatha was about to say they didn't know, but Charles looked at Mrs Darry compassionately and said, 'Oh, yes. We haven't told anyone and Agatha here went to great lengths to try to destroy any evidence that might have incriminated you. That is why we have not gone to the police. We would be in trouble ourselves. Just tell us how he came to get the information.'

'I went there to get my hair done,' said Mrs Darry in a low voice, quite unlike her usual biting tones. 'We got friendly. Had a few meals. I was flattered. I told him that my late husband had been a plumber. A *master* plumber,' she added with some of her old spirit in case he might think he was an ordinary tradesman. 'We were talking about taxes and VAT and how iniquitous both were. He said sympathetically that there were ways round it. He knew a lot of tradesmen who would offer to do a job for a bit less for cash in hand. I'd had a bit too much to drink and so I told him that was what my Clarence had done and so that was the reason I had been left comfortably off.

'Then he phoned me two days later. I couldn't believe it. We were friends! He told me unless I paid him five thousand pounds, he would inform the Inland Revenue that my husband had been cheating them for years. I panicked. I called on him and said that if he did that, I would kill him.' She fell silent. Then she said, 'When I heard he was dead, it was like the end of a nightmare.'

'But look here,' said Agatha. 'When did your husband die?'

'Five years ago.'

'But how on earth could the Inland Revenue find out that he had been taking cash payments and not declaring them?'

'They could have gone to his old customers. I sold the plumbing firm, but they'll still have the old records.'

'But if they were paying cash,' said Agatha patiently, 'those payments would not appear on the books.'

'But what if they found his old customers and asked them?'

'What would they say?' asked Charles. 'They couldn't admit to cheating the income tax either. They'd be in deep shit.'

Weak tears ran down Mrs Darry's face. 'So

it was all for nothing.'

'All what?' asked Agatha sharply.

'All my worry. All my sleepless nights.'

'You didn't kill him?'

'No. I read about it in the papers. Ricin. I'd never even heard of it. Please don't tell the police any of this.'

'I can't,' said Agatha. 'I went to his house to destroy any evidence and someone set it alight. The police don't even know I was there.'

Mrs Darry got up stiffly, as if her joints were hurting. 'I shall make tea,' she said and disappeared into the nether regions.

'You can take the offer of tea as thanks for trying to save her neck,' said Charles.

'It wasn't her scrawny neck I was trying to save but Mrs Friendly's. John really did prey on silly, ugly women who would be flattered by his attentions.'

'And some not so ugly,' said Charles with a slanting look at her.

'I wasn't taken in for a moment!'

'That's not the way I saw it.'

'Never mind that,' said Agatha hurriedly. 'I wonder who inherits. Perhaps all this blackmailing business is clouding the issue. Perhaps he was murdered because of something else.'

'Highly unlikely. Here she comes.'

Mrs Darry returned and proceeded to pour tea that looked like discoloured water. Agatha guessed that she had only used one tea-bag in the pot and probably one that had been used already. There was a plate of hard biscuits.

Mrs Darry seemed to have recovered most of her old composure—or nastiness, as Agatha judged it to be.

'While I was making the tea,' said Mrs Darry, 'I was thinking of your so-called detective abilities. I have a shrewd inquiring mind and I am sure I could find out who did it.'

'You mean you want to work with us?' asked Agatha with a sinking heart.

She gave a pitying laugh. 'Oh, no. As the bard says, she travels fastest who travels alone.'

'It was Kipling,' corrected Charles. '"He travels fastest who travels alone."'

'Whatever.'

Agatha put her teacup down in the saucer with an angry little click. 'Then we will not waste any more of your valuable time.' She got to her feet. Charles rose as well.

'We could compare notes,' said Mrs Darry graciously.

'Oh, but that would surely impede your progress.' Agatha headed resolutely for the door. Charles followed her outside. The dog ran after Agatha and began to snuffle eagerly at her ankles again. She picked it up, placed it inside and firmly shut the door. 'Horrid little thing. Let's get home, Charles, so I can disinfect my contaminated shoe.'

*   *   *

After Agatha had washed her feet and put on clean tights and shoes, she joined Charles in the kitchen and said, 'Portsmouth.'

'What about it?'

'That's where he used to have a business. We could go there and talk to hairdressers and see if there was any scandal about him.'

'Now? What if the police come calling?'

'So what? We're not leaving the country.'

'Do you know Portsmouth? Huge place.'

'We'll get a hotel and look through the *Yellow Pages* and phone up hairdressers.'

'Waste of time, Aggie. We go to Mircester Library and look up the *Yellow Pages* for Portsmouth and phone from here.'

Agatha sighed. 'I suppose you're right. I just wanted to get away.'

'Cheer up. If we find out anything on the phone, then we'll go.'

Just then, the phone rang. It was Mrs Bloxby. 'I think I may have discovered your Maggie for you.'

'Who is she?' said Agatha eagerly. 'Where does she live?'

'I may be wrong but I think you want a Maggie Henderson. She lives at nine, Terrace Road, in Badsey. She's a schoolteacher.'

'How did you find out?'

'I simply gave her description, such as it was, and her first name to various people in the surrounding parishes. It may turn out to be the wrong Maggie.'

'We'll try anyway. Thanks a lot.'

Agatha said goodbye and rang off. She told Charles her news.

'Let's leave Portsmouth just for now and try this Maggie,' he said. 'Badsey's only a few miles away.'

But when they drove to Badsey and found the correct address it was to discover that Maggie Henderson taught at a school at Worcester and was not expected back until about five o'clock. 'And with our luck,' said Agatha gloomily, 'her husband will be home at the same time. Do we go to Worcester?'

'No,' said Charles. 'Let's go into Evesham and find a place for coffee and make notes on what we've got.'

They parked in Merstow Green and walked across the road to a tea-shop off the Market Square. 'Look at this!' exclaimed Charles. 'The last genuine old English tea-shop in captivity.' It was low-beamed, quiet and dark. A waitress with a gentle Scottish accent took their order.

'Now,' said Charles, taking out a small notebook and a pen, 'let's see what we've got in the way of suspects. Begin at the beginning, Aggie. Anything you can think of.'

Agatha rested her chin on her hands. 'Let

134

me see, what made me suspect him of being a blackmailer in the first place? Ah, I know. I told you. I heard some woman threatening to kill him when I was in the loo at the hairdresser's. John said it was a couple in the shop next door who were always quarrelling. But although I could hear her voice, I couldn't distinguish the voice of the man. He kept his low. It could've been John.'

'Right.' He made a note. 'We'll check out that shop afterwards. Next.'

'Wait a bit. He told me he had been married once. That's a thought. I wonder if he had any children and who inherits.'

'We'll try to find out.'

'There was another candidate for blackmail. There was a customer talking to him about her daughter Betty. She said she thought her daughter was not only on drugs but pushing them as well. Her husband was called Jim.'

'Good. More.'

'Then we now know about Mrs Darry, Maggie, and Liza Friendly. Wait a bit. There's Josie.'

'Who's she?'

'Vapid little receptionist. Seemed besotted with John and very jealous of me.'

'Ah,' said Charles, making another note. 'I think I should handle that one. I'll get my hair cut and chat her up. That way I can pick up the gossip about the customers.'

135

'Then,' said Agatha, 'do you remember how Liza was telling us about watching the house and she saw this blonde? How did she describe her? Blonde, I think, rabbity, prominent teeth, skinny legs. I think that's all we've got.'

'So there's one of these suspects or maybe someone we haven't heard of who had the keys to his house. Remember, you didn't hear anyone breaking in . . . unless . . . Oh, why didn't we think of the obvious?'

'What?'

'I bet when you let yourself in you didn't lock the door behind you.'

Agatha goggled at him.

'Think!' urged Charles. 'Was it a Yale, the kind that would automatically click shut and lock behind you?'

'No,' said Agatha slowly. 'It was a mortise. Biggish key.'

'Then that explains that.'

Agatha clutched his arm. 'Don't you see, if someone knew just to walk in, they must have known I was in there!'

'Could be. Or maybe someone just tried the handle first and meant to break in if the door was locked. Did it have glass panes?'

'Yes, those stained-glass ones. You know, Charles, I think we might be concentrating too hard on the blackmailing angle.'

'What other angle is there?'

'Oh, passion and jealousy. Jealous woman,

jealous husband. Remember, someone did beat him up.'

'Stick to blackmail,' said Charles in an authoritative manner which made Agatha long to prove him wrong.

'If you've finished,' said Agatha huffily, 'let's try that shop next door to the hairdresser's. Wait a bit. Surely the hairdresser's will be closed down?'

'Damn, of course it will be.'

'Let's take a look anyway.'

They walked along the High Street. Sure enough, the hairdresser's was closed and dark.

'We'll try the shop next door,' said Charles.

They both entered a small dark shop which sold an assortment of cheap souvenirs.

There was an enormous woman behind the counter dressed in a man's shirt and leggings. They could see the leggings because she was bending over to pick up something from the bottom shelves behind the counter.

'Excuse me,' began Agatha. The woman straightened up and turned round.

She had a large, round, truculent face and thick glasses. 'What d'ye want?' she snapped.

Agatha, accustomed to the usual friendly manners of the Evesham shopkeeper, blinked and said, 'We wondered whether you knew that man next door who was murdered?'

'And what's it to do with you? You're not the police. Who are you? More of those ghouls who want to gossip about the murder

137

and not buy anything?'

Agatha took the plunge. 'I heard you threatening to kill Mr John.'

Her large face was a study in surprise. 'I never did! When's this supposed to have happened?'

'I was in the toilet at the hairdresser's a few weeks ago. I asked John Shawpart about it and he said you and your husband were always quarrelling.'

The woman held up a large, pudgy, ringless hand. 'Ain't got a husband. Come with me.' She lifted the flap of the counter. They walked through. She led them through to a grimy kitchen in the back shop. She opened the kitchen door. 'Look!'

There was only a narrow little strip of yard. On the hairdresser's side was a high wall. 'On the other side of that wall is the hairdresser's yard,' she said. 'Whoever you heard, it couldn't have been me. You heard someone out in the yard of the hairdresser's.'

The bell tinkled in the shop. 'Got a customer,' she said. 'Get out of here.'

'What do you think?' asked Charles when they were back out in the High Street.

'I think Mr John lied, that's what I think,' said Agatha. 'I say, that's a new hairdresser's across the road. Eve's, it says. And look through the window.'

'What?'

'At the desk. It's that receptionist, Josie.'

'Then take yourself off somewhere, Aggie, and let me go and get my hair cut and chat her up.'

'How long will you be?'

'Give me an hour. Here's the car keys. I'll meet you back at the car park.'

'I tell you what. You go in and after a few moments, I'll go in myself and make an appointment. Maybe all the old staff are there.'

Agatha waited impatiently while Charles crossed the road and went in. He spent some time talking to Josie, who was giggling and laughing. Then he disappeared into the nether regions.

Agatha crossed the road. Josie was still smiling, but the smile left her face when she saw Agatha. 'So this is where you are,' said Agatha brightly. Within the salon she saw Garry and two other of Mr John's former assistants.

'Yes, we was lucky. Eve opened up and she took us all on.'

'Who's Eve?'

Josie gave an impertinent sigh and bent over the appointments book. 'Do you want to make an appointment, Mrs Raisin? We're very busy.'

Agatha opened her mouth to blast her and then thought better of it. 'Put me down for the day after tomorrow. Three o'clock.'

'Do you want Garry?'

139

'No, I'll try Eve herself.'

'It'll need to be four o'clock.'

'Okay, that'll do.'

Agatha walked out again into the High Street. She wandered about Evesham, down Bridge Street to the Abbey Gardens, sat and smoked and then made her way to Charles's car to find him standing outside, waiting for her.

'How did you get on?'

He took the keys from her and unlocked the car.

'I'll tell you on the road to Badsey.'

When they drove off, he started, 'I'm taking Josie out for dinner tonight. I gather that this new hairdresser came along and employed them all. Hard-looking woman. But fast. She has them all working—snipping and perming and tinting as if they're all on an assembly line. Josie is going to tell me all.'

'Do you think this new hairdresser might have bumped off Mr John to get his trade?'

'What a fertile imagination you have, Aggie. This isn't Sunday night viewing on telly. This is real life. We have a dead blackmailer. So it is perfectly logical to assume that someone murdered him to get him out of their threatened life.'

'Well, we'll see what Maggie has to say,' said Agatha gloomily. 'She's probably another woman with a truculent husband.'

'Her car's outside, anyway,' said Charles as

they drove up. 'If it is her car and not her husband's.'

They got out and walked up an ankle-spraining front path made of pieces of brick. The garden was neglected and weedy and the net curtains at the windows were dingy.

Agatha pressed the doorbell. 'No ring,' said Charles. 'Knock.'

Agatha rapped on the glass panes of the door. I wonder why anyone ever becomes a newspaper reporter, she thought. They condemn themselves to days of rejection.

The door opened on a chain and one of Maggie's protuberant eyes stared at them.

Agatha smiled brightly. 'Do you remember me, Mrs Henderson? We met in the hairdressing salon, Mr John's, in Evesham.'

'What do you want?'

'We wanted to talk to you about Mr John.'

'I've nothing to say.'

'We know he was blackmailing you,' said Charles.

The door slammed. Agatha and Charles looked at each other.

Then they heard the sound of the chain being dropped and the door opened.

Maggie Henderson looked at them triumphantly. 'You can't do anything to me now. I suppose you got hold of the letters that bastard had. Well, the damage is done. My husband's left me, so go screw yourselves.'

'We're not blackmailers,' said Agatha. 'Can

we come in? All the evidence is destroyed.'

'In the fire?'

Agatha nodded. 'The reason I want to find out who killed him and who set the house on fire is that I was in the house when it was set alight. I went there to try to destroy any evidence. But don't tell the police that. They don't know.'

Maggie's face softened. 'So you were a victim as well. Come in.'

'Not really . . .' began Agatha, but Charles pressed her arm warningly as they followed Maggie into the house, as if to say, let her think you're a fellow sufferer.

The living-room was untidy and dusty. 'I had a call from a policewoman,' said Maggie. 'Sit down. She was only checking her way through the list of customers and when I read that his house had burned down, I prayed my letters had gone up with it. I thought, you see, with all the rain that day that they might not, but the policewoman told me that he had used Calor gas and kept spare cylinders in the basement. The gas exploded. She said even the stuff in the filing cabinet had been destroyed.'

I didn't even see the filing cabinet, thought Agatha.

'So what happened between you and Mr John?' she asked. 'I am Agatha Raisin and this is Sir Charles Fraith.'

'Well, Mrs Raisin . . .'

'Call me Agatha.'

'That's a name you don't hear much these days,' said Maggie. 'I had a friend called Agatha but she changed her name to Helen. Said she couldn't bear people calling her Aggie.'

'I know how she feels,' said Agatha, casting a fulminating glance at Charles.

'I was so glad when I heard he was dead,' said Maggie. 'I could've murdered him. But I'm such a rabbit. Things weren't going too well in my marriage. Pete was a good husband, I suppose, but always a dab hand at nasty little putting-down remarks. Any time we went out to the pub with friends, I knew there would be a post-mortem on the road home. "Why did you say that, you made a fool of yourself, you looked like a tart," that sort of thing. But that's marriage for you. Then Mr John started to ask me out, meetings on the sly. Pete was out at work and I was enjoying the school holidays. He made me feel like a princess. I began to complain about Pete to him. He was very sympathetic. He said a lot of women were stuck in lousy marriages because they hadn't the funds to leave. I said I had always had my own money. My parents died in a car crash and left me comfortably off. He exhilarated me. I saw for the first time that it might be possible to find the courage to leave Pete. This is my house.'

She fell silent.

143

'Then what happened?' prompted Agatha.

'He made love to me and I felt beautiful.' Agatha felt a slight pang of regret that she hadn't given the hairdresser a fling. 'Then, after that, he was suddenly too busy to see me or even to do my hair. I was obsessed, frantic. The school holidays were coming to an end and I knew I wouldn't have much freedom. So I wrote to him, reminding him of our love, of our afternoon of love.

'When he said he wanted to see me again, I was overjoyed. We met at those tea gardens on the river. He told me he wanted money, five thousand pounds. If I didn't give it to him, he would send my letter to my husband. I hated him in that moment. I didn't believe for a minute he would do it. So I told him to do his worst.

'I felt guilty about the way I had cheated on Pete over this useless, evil man. The next day, the very next day, Pete was off work with a cold. The post hadn't arrived when I went out to work. So Pete got the letter. John must have posted it right after I left him the day before.

'When I got home, Pete had packed up and left. My letter was on the table and Pete left me his own letter, calling me all sorts of names . . . slut, whore.' Her voice broke.

'I'm so lonely without him. I never thought I would be. I used to dream day and night of getting my freedom and now I've got it, and it sucks.'

She began to cry.

Agatha handed her a pile of tissues from a box on the dusty table. Maggie blew her nose and wiped her eyes.

'Where is your husband now?' asked Charles.

'Over at his mother's in Honeybourne.'

'Did either you or your husband go to the police?'

'Oh, no! I burnt my letter and Pete's. And when I read about the murder I was frantic. I thought Pete had done it. But it was poisoning and Pete would have been more likely to club him to death. My Pete has a violent temper.'

'Perhaps we should have a word with your husband,' suggested Charles, thinking of Agatha's description of the bruised face.

Agatha expected Maggie to exclaim in horror, but she pressed her trembling hands together and said, 'If you could. He won't speak to me and his mother takes all the calls and refuses to let me speak to him. Tell him I miss him. I mean, he wasn't much company, but he was good at fixing things.'

'Give us the address,' said Charles, 'and we'll see what we can do.'

'It's ten, Parton Lane, Honeybourne. But you mustn't tell the police about me! I'm falling apart as it is. All I want is Pete back. You never know what you've got until you haven't got it any more.'

If only James Lacey thought like that, mourned Agatha.

As Charles and Agatha got in the car again, Charles looked at his watch and said, 'Can't be too long on this next call. I've got to take Josie out for dinner.'

'We've got time,' said Agatha. 'Honeybourne's not far.'

They found the address quite easily. 'Here goes,' said Charles.

The door was answered by a small, bent woman who peered up at them from under a thatch of grey hair.

'Mrs Henderson?' said Agatha.

'Yes, and I'm not interested in buying anything.'

'We're not selling anything.'

'We've come to see your son,' said Charles.

'Who are you?'

'Mrs Agatha Raisin and Sir Charles Fraith.'

She scowled at them suspiciously and then retreated into the house. There was the sound of some altercation from the nether regions and then a large burly man filled the doorway. 'Yes?' he demanded truculently.

How easy it would be to be a police detective, thought Agatha. Flash the identification and demand that they go indoors.

'It's about that hairdresser, John Shawpart,' said Agatha.

'What the hell's it got to do with you?'

'We wondered why you had beaten him up,' said Charles, edging in front of Agatha.

'You the police?'

'No, we became involved in the case.'

Pete Henderson roundly told Charles to go and perform an impossible anatomical act upon himself. The door began to close.

'Maggie misses you,' said Agatha desperately. 'She really does.'

The door stopped closing.

'It's her own fault,' said Pete. 'Slut.'

'It was only one mistake,' cajoled Agatha.

'Serves her right,' he growled. 'Did she think any man would be interested in her? She should have known he was a blackmailer.'

'But she was tricked,' said Agatha. 'Now she misses you and she's frantic with worry.'

A gleam of satisfaction replaced the anger in his eyes.

'I hope she's suffering,' he said and slammed the door in their faces.

'Well, what did we get from that?' asked Agatha as they drove off.

'I think we can be pretty sure he's the one that beat John Shawpart up. Better run you home, Aggie. Got to meet Josie.'

'I'll wait up for you to hear your news.'

'Well . . .'

'You wouldn't, Charles! A young girl like that!'

'Don't worry. She probably lives with her parents.'

147

                    *   *   *

After Charles had left, Agatha planned to have a peaceful evening but Worcester CID called and took her through her statement, demanding this time to know why she had lied about driving past Shawpart's house. Wearily Agatha said it was because murder made everyone feel guilty and she had not wanted to sound like one of those ghouls who haunt the scenes of disasters. By the time they left, she felt almost as if she had committed the murder herself.

She had a hot bath and put on a night-dress and dressing-gown and sat in front of the television set, waiting for Charles to come home. She sometimes wondered if Charles regarded her as anything more than a sort of amusement to enliven his days. He was as neat and self-contained as a cat. Although he had temporarily moved in with her, he did not seem to take up any space at all.

It was around midnight, when she was just falling asleep in the armchair, that she heard him driving up.

She struggled to her feet and opened the door.

'Not trying to seduce me, are you, Aggie?' was Charles's greeting as he surveyed her plain and serviceable dressing-gown worn over a high-necked cotton night-dress.

'Come in and tell me about it.'

Agatha led the way into the living-room and quickly switched off the television, where a rerun of *Star Trek* was showing, in case Charles decided to watch it.

Charles poured himself a drink and sat down.

'I've found out the identity of the slim, rabbity blonde.'

'Who is she?'

He brought out his small notebook. 'Jessie Lang. Evesham girl. Josie said bitterly that she came in one day and made a hell of a scene.'

'What about?'

'Seems he stood her up.'

'Another unhappily married woman?'

'No, she works as a dentist's receptionist, isn't married and doesn't appear to be well off.'

'Got her address?'

'No, Josie said the police have the old appointments book and it only had phone numbers in it anyway. But she works at a dentist's in the High Street. I've got the address. God, I'm tired. We'll go tomorrow.'

'Anything else?'

'Well, our Josie was smitten by her boss, that's for sure, but I gather she never got anywhere. She seemed ready to turn her affections on me.'

'And what did you tell her?'

'I said I loved only you. Fortunately, that

was over coffee, for the evening promptly went down the tubes.'

'What did she say to that?'

'You don't want to know.' Josie had actually exclaimed, 'What, that old frump!'

'What about Portsmouth?' fretted Agatha.

'It can wait a bit. The action's here, Aggie.'

'I wish you wouldn't call me that! I think the action began in Portsmouth. What if he blackmailed his customers there and one of them followed him up here? Oh, Worcester CID called when you were out. Nag, nag, nag. Same old questions, apart from the fact they'd found out I was lying about just hearing John's house had gone on fire. Made me feel guilty.'

'So what should we do at the dentist's tomorrow?' asked Charles. 'March in and question her there?'

'No, she's bound to go out for lunch. We know what she looks like. We'll go in about lunchtime and waylay her.'

'She might have lunch at her desk. I suggest I use my charm and invite her out for lunch. You could fill in the time by getting your hair done.'

'I've got an appointment with that Eve person, but it's for four o'clock, the day after tomorrow.'

'See if you can change it.'

'I should think the terrible Josie will delight in telling me that there are no free appointments, but I'll try. I'll phone in the morning. Oh, I forgot to check when we got back from Honeybourne if there were any messages.'

Agatha went to the phone and dialled. She listened and then put down the phone and turned to Charles. 'A message from Mrs Darry. She says she wants to see me. She sounded like her old self. Nasty and bitchy. I'll think about it. Maybe call on her when we've finished in Evesham.'

*　　　*　　　*

The following day, Agatha left Charles outside the dentist's and went to the hairdresser's. Josie was barely polite but reluctantly said there was a cancellation. Agatha had her hair shampooed and was led through to Eve.

Eve was a tall, stately woman, rather like a figurehead on an old ship, proud bosom, flowing dark hair, rounded arms.

As she worked away with the drier, Agatha said, 'Did you know Mr John?'

'The hairdresser who was killed? No. Terribly sad, that,' said Eve. 'Lucky for me. I was starting up this business and about to advertise for staff, so I just took his old staff over. I think I'll just pop some rollers in and put you under the drier. Gives it a firmer set.'

'I don't want anything too fussy!'

'Oh, it'll look great.'

'Are you from Evesham, Eve?'

'No, I moved here recently. Thought it might be a good place for business.'

'Where were you before?'

'Worcester.'

Agatha fell silent as the hairdresser put down the drier and then rolled her hair up and sprayed it.

'Yvette, put Agatha under the drier,' called Eve.

'Terrible about Mr John,' said Agatha to Yvette.

'Yeah. Want some magazines?'

Agatha nodded. The drier was lowered over her head. Several copies of last year's *Vogue* and *Good Housekeeping* were plopped on her lap. At first Agatha amused herself by reading last year's horoscopes to see if they were anything like what had happened to her, but, like most horoscopes, they were so vague you could read anything you wanted into them.

Time passed. Agatha squinted at her watch. Her hair had been nearly dry when it had been put in the rollers and she had been under the wretched drier for nearly an hour.

Determinedly she put the magazines on a table beside her, removed her head from the drier and went through to the salon.

No sign of Eve.

'Where is she?' barked Agatha.

'Gone out for her lunch,' said Garry, who

was perming a customer's hair.

'What kind of place is this?' howled Agatha. 'I want my hair finished now!'

Garry threw her a frightened look. 'She's in the restaurant next door. I'll get her.'

Agatha stood and fumed. Eve came hurrying back in.

'In a rush, are we?' she asked sweetly.

'I don't know about you, but I do not like to be kept waiting,' snapped Agatha.

'Well, I'm here now,' said Eve soothingly. She guided Agatha to a chair and began to remove the rollers. Then she back-combed and smoothed the hair.

Agatha stared at her reflection in the mirror.

'That,' she said bitterly, 'is the epitome of provincial middle-aged hair-styles. Too bouffant.'

'It's the latest style,' said Eve.

'It was the latest style somewhere around the sixties.'

'If you would like me to restyle it?'

'Oh, forget it. Just give me the bill and let me out of here.'

In a thoroughly bad temper, Agatha went back to the car park to wait for Charles. Fortunately for her, they had used her car, so she sat and smoked and waited . . . and waited.

Eventually Charles turned up.

He burst out laughing when he saw Agatha's hair. 'Oh, shut up,' snarled Agatha.

'I'll never go there again. Take her for lunch while I sat here and starved?'

'No, our Jessie was very frightened. Said she had not known our Mr John, refused to talk about him.'

'So what kept you?'

'I went for lunch.'

'Why didn't you come looking for me?'

'I didn't think. I was hungry.'

'I'm going straight home to brush out this wretched style and eat. You can do what you like.'

'Since you're driving,' said Charles mildly, 'whither thou goest, I goest.'

Agatha grumbled the whole way back to Carsely about the sheer selfishness of men.

Once home, she was restored to good temper by two chicken sandwiches and a cup of soup and by brushing her hair smooth.

'Now what?' she asked. 'Perhaps I should have been the one to have a go at Jessie Lang.'

'You can have a try. What about Mrs Darry?'

'God, I'd forgotten about her. Let's take a walk up there. She's probably regretted telling us anything.'

'All right. You know, Aggie, if that ricin was put into his vitamin pills, it could have been done at any time. All the poisoner had to do was wait. You know what I mean? Poison two of them and you could be out of the country by the time he got to them.'

Agatha sighed. 'I'm beginning to wonder if we'll ever find out who did it.'

'Anyway, let's see what Mrs Darry has to say for herself.'

*   *   *

The day was cold and grey as they walked through the village. The first leaves of autumn twirled down at their feet. 'All that heat seems so far away now,' said Agatha. 'I don't like the winter in the country. You really never notice it in town. Afternoon, terrible weather, isn't it?'

'Who was that woman you just spoke to?'

'I don't know,' said Agatha. 'Apart from the women who go to the ladies' society, I don't really know that many people in the village. In Carsely, we all say "Morning" or "Afternoon" to each other, whether we know each other or not.'

'What about the community spirit?'

'I think it went when everyone got cars,' said Agatha. 'The children are bussed out to schools and a lot of the parents work up in Birmingham or Worcester and commute. Here we are now. I can't help hoping she's not at home.'

The little cottage lay dark and silent. 'That's her car,' said Agatha. 'She's probably walking the dog. Don't peer in the window,

Charles. I tell you, she's out. Charles!'

He turned round and looked at her, his face strangely pinched and drawn.

'Aggie, there's a pair of feet sticking out from behind the sofa.'

'She must be ill. Let's try the door.'

Agatha turned the brass handle on the front door. It swung open. Agatha rushed into the living-room. Mrs Darry lay stretched out behind the sofa. Blood from a terrible wound on her head spread out on the carpet. Beside her lay the corpse of her little dog, and beside both lay a blood-stained brass poker.

Charles knelt down beside Mrs Darry, feeling for a pulse and finding none.

He shook his head dismally. Agatha dialled 999 and asked for the police and an ambulance.

She turned to Charles. 'I think I'm going to be sick.'

'Better go outside on the road.'

Agatha fled. She was thoroughly sick. She tried to brace herself to return to Charles but found she hadn't the courage to go back into the house of death. Somehow it was the memory of the little dog with its head smashed in as well that made the picture that was imprinted on her mind so full of horror. It had been murder done in a vicious rage. Murder done in Carsely. Murder coming closer to Agatha Raisin.

Fred Griggs, the village policeman, came

hurrying up. Agatha told him in a weak, faltering voice what had happened. He went into the house.

Then two police cars arrived; Bill Wong, Detective Inspector Wilkes and various other plain-clothes detectives and police officers. Then the ambulance.

Agatha waited, shivering.

At last Bill Wong came out. 'I'll take you home, Agatha. You look awful.'

'It's my hair,' babbled Agatha insanely. 'That wretched hairdresser ruined my hair.'

'Get in the police car. You'll feel better when you've had a cup of tea.'

Back at her cottage and despite her protests that she couldn't drink anything, Bill made her a cup of milky sweet tea. 'Try to get it down you. You'll feel better.'

'If only I'd gone to see her last night,' mourned Agatha.

'Why? Why last night? What do you know?'

'I may as well tell you now she's dead. She was being blackmailed by that hairdresser, Mr John.'

'Drink some tea and begin at the beginning.'

Agatha did as she was bid and then in a halting voice told him about Mrs Darry.

When she had finished, he demanded, 'Did you tell Worcester CID any of this?'

She shook her head.

'Why not? Perhaps she would still be alive if

157

you had. I've warned you and warned you about the danger of playing amateur detective.'

'It was told to me in confidence.'

'Is there anything else you haven't told the police?'

Agatha longed to unburden herself, but she could not betray Liza or Maggie. Besides, would either woman have been capable of committing such a savage and violent act of murder?

'No,' she lied. 'Nothing.'

A voice in her brain screamed that any woman frightened of exposure as a murderess might kill again in a frenzy of rage, but she hung her head and stared at the floor.

'I'll need to get back,' said Bill. 'We'll be along later to take a statement. Why did you call on her?'

'She left a message on my Call Minder.'

'Saying what?'

'Just that she wanted to see me. She sounded as bad-tempered and bitchy as usual.'

'Wait here.'

Bill left. Agatha sat hugging herself. A stiff wind had risen and moaned in the thatch.

The door opened and Charles came in. She rose and threw herself into his arms. 'It's horrible, Charles. Let's leave it to the police. Let's forget about the whole thing.'

'There, now. Brace up. They'll all be along in a minute. I gather you told Bill Wong about

Shawpart attempting to blackmail Mrs Darry. You didn't tell him about the others?'

'No.'

'Neither did I. So we wait. We'll not only have Gloucester police grilling us but Worcester as well because of the Shawpart connection. It's going to be a long day, Aggie.'

* * *

And it was. They were both driven to police headquarters in Worcester and grilled again.

Agatha felt shaky and sick. Finally, they were released with a stern warning not to interfere in police business.

'Drink?' said Charles.

Agatha shivered. 'I just want to go home.'

'Hey, we came here in a police car. How do the rats expect us to get back? Let's go and ask them for a car.'

'We'll get a taxi. I'm not going back in there.'

'Aggie, this is Worcester. It'll cost us a lot. Let them do it.'

'I'll pay.'

They sat silently side by side in the cab going home. Then Agatha broke the silence as they were nearing Carsely by asking, 'Do you feel anything about all this, Charles? I mean, you seem very cool.'

'It was nasty, but I just put it out of my head.'

159

'I wish I could be like you,' mourned Agatha. 'I think I'll see poor Mrs Darry lying there until the day I die.'

'Come on. You didn't even like her.'

'It doesn't mitigate the horror.'

'Does for me,' remarked Charles with what Agatha thought was truly heartless indifference.

Indoors, he poured drinks for both of them and lit the fire, which had fortunately been cleaned out by Agatha's help, Doris Simpson, who was once more back on the job.

Charles settled down to read the newspapers which had been delivered that morning.

'Listen to this, Aggie,' he said, rustling the paper. 'It says in this report, "A fleck of dandruff, a licked stamp or a smudged fingerprint on a car key could soon be used by scientists to catch and convict criminals. Researchers have developed a method of DNA fingerprinting which will work with a single human cell." Didn't shed any dandruff around Shawpart's house, did you?'

'I don't have dandruff,' said Agatha crossly, 'and anyway, the police know I visited him although I didn't tell them I was there when the fire started. So what?'

'Let's eat.'

'I couldn't.'

Charles threw down the paper. 'I'll make us something. Got to keep your strength up.'

After fifteen minutes, he called Agatha into the kitchen. 'Cup of soup and cheese omelette. Get it down you.'

Agatha found to her surprise that she was hungry.

They tried to watch television after dinner, but Agatha finally said, 'I think I'll have an early night.'

'Good idea.'

*   *   *

Agatha found she could not sleep. Every time she closed her eyes, she saw Mrs Darry and the dog lying in their own blood.

She got out of bed and went to Charles's room. He was lying awake, reading.

'I can't sleep,' said Agatha. 'I've got the horrors.'

'Come and join me and cuddle up.'

She climbed into bed next to him. He held her close and then began to kiss her hair.

'Charles,' protested Agatha, 'I didn't come for . . .'

Chapter Six

Agatha awoke in the morning to find Charles gone. She stretched and yawned and then remembered the night's love-making as if it had all happened in a dream. But the sun was shining outside and the horrors had gone.

She went down to the kitchen. Charles had left a note: 'Just remembered I've got guests arriving. Phone you later, Charles.'

It wouldn't have hurt him to have said something affectionate, thought Agatha. She went back upstairs and washed and dressed and came down just as the doorbell rang. For the first time, she did not hope it was James. It must be Charles. With a glad smile, she flung open the door.

Mrs Bloxby stood there. Agatha's face fell. 'Oh, it's you. Come in.'

'Who were you expecting?'

'Charles. You've heard about the murder? Of course you have. It was dreadful. Absolutely dreadful. Did she have any family?'

'She has a daughter and son,' said Mrs Bloxby. 'They are with the police at the moment.'

Agatha told her all about Mrs Darry, about the attempted blackmail, and how Mrs Darry had said she was going to play detective herself.

'But she couldn't have got very far,' exclaimed the vicar's wife. 'Unless, of course, she had known John Shawpart somewhere before. Where was he before he came to Evesham?'

'Portsmouth. He said Portsmouth. I might drive there today and see what I can find out.'

'So who are your suspects?'

'I don't think we have any except perhaps either Mrs Friendly's husband or Maggie Henderson's husband. There is a certain Jessie Lang who works at a dentist's in Evesham who knew him and was seen at his house. Oh, and John told me he had been married once. Damn, the police probably know who to and where but they won't tell me.'

'And where is Charles today?' asked Mrs Bloxby brightly—too brightly, thought Agatha as those mild eyes studied her face.

'Oh, he's got guests. He'll probably be back later.' Did he pack? wondered Agatha suddenly.

'Of course, I don't think it can be a man,' said Mrs Bloxby.

'Why?'

'Just a feeling.'

'I don't know. Of course poisoning is traditionally a woman's weapon.'

'In history, a lot of the famous poisoners were actually men—Neill Cream, Carlyle

163

Harris, Roland B. Molineux, Henri Landru, and so on.'

Agatha sighed. 'I keep forgetting that fire. Whoever set that fire killed John; I'm sure of it. Where was Mrs Darry living before she came here?'

Mrs Bloxby frowned in concentration. Then she shook her head. 'She told me, but I can't remember at the moment. It'll come back to me. I think perhaps you should leave this to the police. That killing of Mrs Darry was savage. Perhaps it might be wise if you went away for a bit. If the murderer is one of the people you've already talked to, they might come after you.'

'I'll try just a little bit longer. In villages, people are supposed to know everyone else's comings and goings. It's a wonder no one was seen going to Mrs Darry's cottage.'

'Ah, but our local bobby, Fred, told me the police think whoever it was entered from the back. If someone went round by the back lane, they wouldn't be seen. No other cottages overlook the back.'

'Someone broke in?'

Mrs Bloxby shook her head. 'They think she knew her caller. She had already served tea before she was struck down. Didn't you notice that? But she always left her doors unlocked when she was at home.'

'All I saw was her shattered head and that poor dog.' Agatha shivered. Why hadn't

164

Charles phoned?

'Please don't do anything more about it.' The vicar's wife looked worried. 'I really do believe it will put you in danger.'

'I'll just ask around a bit.' And maybe it was a good idea to get away from Carsely, thought Agatha. Serve Charles right if he called and found her gone.

*   *   *

After lunch, a restless Agatha decided to drive to Worcester and present herself at police headquarters to see if they might tell her how far they had got.

She drove into Evesham and turned on to the Pershore Road just before the bridge. She glanced across the road at the river. People were fishing and other people were watching them. Then she jammed on the brakes and pulled into the side of the road. An infuriated truck driver roared past, flashing his lights.

Agatha peered across the road, but her view was blocked by traffic. She eased out, drove on, found a convenient place to turn and headed back. For she had seen a blonde, rabbity-looking girl watching the fishing and all at once she was sure that girl was Jessie Lang.

By the time she had parked in the meadows and set out on foot, she had begun to think that Evesham was probably full of blonde, rabbity-looking girls. Still, it was worth a try.

She approached the place where she thought she had seen the girl who looked like Jessie. No sign of her. No sign of any blonde. Men fished. People watched them. Children ran around screaming. Children always screamed these days, thought Agatha sourly.

And then, farther along the tow-path, she saw a blonde head bobbing along. She hurried and when she was nearly up to her, she called, 'Jessie!'

The girl stopped and turned around. Yes, there were the rabbity teeth and skinny legs.

Agatha smiled and held out her hand. 'Jessie Lang? I'm Agatha Raisin.'

The girl touched Agatha's hand with her own skeletal one. 'Who are you? I don't know you. Are you one of the patients?'

'No, I'm investigating the murder of John Shawpart,' Agatha blurted out.

Jessie backed away, fear darting into her eyes. 'Are you the police?'

Agatha knew in that moment that if she said she was a private individual, the girl would run away from her.

She took out her credit-card case and snapped it quickly open and shut. 'Detective Constable Raisin,' said Agatha. 'Shall we sit over there and have a few words?'

She led the way to a bench. The girl followed her, stumbling as her high heels spiked into the grass.

They sat down side by side.

'We know,' said Agatha, 'that you were seen visiting John Shawpart at his house.'

Jessie began to cry. 'My m-mum'll kill me,' she sobbed.

'We do not need to bring your mother or any of your family into this,' said Agatha. 'Just tell the truth and you've got nothing to fear. Here.' She opened her capacious handbag and drew out a packet of tissues.

Jessie blew her nose and wiped her eyes. 'Sure Mum won't get to know?'

'I see no reason why she should.'

Jessie took a deep breath. 'Mum doesn't like me, see. She's always been picking on me. My sister Rachel's the favourite. If Mum knew, she'd tell my boyfriend, Wayne. She's like that, Mum is.'

'So what happened?'

'He come on to me, John did.'

'When? Where? In the salon?'

'No, at the disco off Bridge Street.'

'A disco? I thought he would have been a bit old for a disco.'

She hiccuped and gave a pathetic little sniff. 'That's what my pals thought. Wayne was away. He's a long-distance driver, so I was there with the girls and they was giggling about him. But I thought he looked like a film star. He saw me clocking him and he come over and offered to buy me a drink. We got talking. He was flash, y'know. He asked me if

I'd like to meet him for dinner the following night and Wayne was still away and I thought then it was a bit of a giggle, so I said yes.'

She fell silent. Children played, mothers gossiped, the river Avon chuckled past between its grassy banks. A pleasure boat like the one Agatha and Charles had sailed on cruised past. Charles, why didn't you phone?

'So then what happened?'

'It was ever such a posh restaurant and we drank a lot and one thing led to another.'

'You slept with him?' What a euphemism, thought Agatha bleakly, remembering the previous night.

'Yes,' she whispered. 'And I was a virgin. I was saving meself for Wayne.'

'How old are you?'

'Twenty.'

Oh, God, I could kill him myself were the bastard still alive, thought Agatha fiercely.

Aloud she asked, 'How long did the affair go on?'

Her thin hands twisted together. 'That was it. He never took me out again. I called at his house. He said it was a one-night stand I should have known that. I told him he had taken my virginity and he said, "So what? You're old enough to lose it." I could've killed him.' Her eyes dilated. 'But I didn't!'

'Are you sure Wayne doesn't know about this?'

She shook her head. 'My pals teased him

about some fellow at the disco buying me a drink, but they said he was old.'

'Did you know we believe John Shawpart to have been a blackmailer?'

She shook her head.

Agatha patted her hand. 'Don't worry. I'm amazed that a girl of your age these days should still be a virgin.'

Jessie gave a wry smile. 'You oldies all think we're at it like rabbits, but I was saving myself for Wayne, just like in those Barbara Cartland books. I'll need to tell Wayne.'

'Is he very experienced?'

'He's a virgin like I was before that sodding hairdresser got me.'

Well, well, God bless Evesham, the last home of innocence, thought Agatha.

She said aloud, 'Look, I don't think you've given us anything we can use. We're only interested in the people he was blackmailing. As one woman to another, I'll do this for you; I won't tell my bosses I've met you.'

'Oh, thank you. What was your name again?'

'It doesn't matter,' said Agatha, a small feeling of panic beginning to enter her brain. What if the police did catch up with this girl and learned she had been impersonating a police officer!

'You're ever so kind,' said Jessie, her face now radiant with relief.

Agatha walked quickly away. But what,

niggled a voice in her brain, just what if Wayne knew about it and took revenge? I should have asked for Wayne's address, but then I can't ask now. I've done enough damage by pretending to be a detective. I hope to God I never run into her in Evesham. I hope she never learns that I've got nothing to do with the police.

She felt a weariness when she walked back to her car. How pleasant it would be to forget about the whole thing and sit in the meadows and watch the placid river flowing past. Evesham people did not seem to be plagued with ambition. Yes, that's it, Agatha Raisin! It's just ambition. You want to prove to the police you can do better.

Then she thought, what about that woman who was complaining about her daughter, Betty, pushing drugs? Her husband was called Jim. How to find out? Not from Josie. Damn Charles, he should have asked her about it. There was Garry, however. If she made an appointment with Garry, she could maybe get something out of him.

She had not tipped him that time he had done her hair, she had been so cross with the result. She could go in and, if he was free, start off by apologizing for her previous lapse and tip him generously. Agatha decided to forget about going to Worcester.

She drove to the Merstow Green car park and then walked along the High Street to

Eve's. Eve was perming a woman's hair. Apart from that, there were no other customers in the shop.

Josie looked at Agatha with barely concealed animosity.

'Is Garry free?' asked Agatha.

'I'll get him,' said Josie ungraciously.

She disappeared into the back premises and then came back followed by Garry.

'I just happen to have a cancellation,' said Garry brightly. He swirled a gown around Agatha and led her through to the wash-basins. No juniors, Agatha noticed. Had they been sacked due to lack of business? She fumbled under her gown and drew a fiver out of the pocket of her jacket. 'Here, I forgot to tip you last time.'

'Thanks a lot,' said Garry, visibly brightening.

'Very quiet today,' said Agatha. 'I just want a blow-dry, please.'

Garry looked around and then bent over her. 'Don't know what's happening. All Mr John's customers came here at first.'

'Are they going somewhere else?'

'I think they're going to Thomas Oliver down the street.'

'Got a good reputation, have they?'

'Never been in there.'

Agatha waited until her hair was washed and she was led through into the salon. Eve was heading out of the door. 'Won't be long,

Garry,' she said curtly. 'Mind the store.'

'There she goes,' he said. 'You'd think she might wait around a bit. Sometimes customers walk in off the street.'

'You don't seem to be enjoying yourself much here,' said Agatha sympathetically.

'It's dead boring. Too quiet.' He raised the blow-drier.

'Mr John's always seemed to be full of people and gossip,' Agatha said. 'And the things they said! I remember hearing a woman talking about her husband, Jim, and her daughter Betty. She even said that she thought her daughter might be pushing drugs.'

'Oh, that'd be Mavis Burke. You have to take everything she says with a pinch of salt.'

'Local woman?'

'Yes, lives in one of those new houses on the Four Pools Estate.' He switched on the drier and began to work busily.

I can't ask him if he knows the address, thought Agatha. That would be pushing it. I'll go to the post office and check the phone book for Burkes.

She suffered dismally under the ministrations of the energetic Garry. He had been bad enough before, but now he was worse. She looked sadly at her bouffant hair-style.

'Very nice,' she said bleakly. She tipped him again, paid Josie and went out into the High Street.

She went into a phone-box at the post office and checked her Call Minder. 'No messages,' said the tinny, elocuted voice, with what Agatha felt was smug satisfaction. So face up to it. Charles had laid her and now he was gone and she was on her own.

She asked at the counter for the Worcestershire phone book and ran her finger down the Burkes. There was one Burke on the Four Pools Estate, and J. Burke at that.

I'll show Charles, I'll show the police, I'll show *everybody* I can do it on my own. Agatha strode along the High Street to the car park. She caught a glimpse of her reflection in a shop window and shuddered. The things I suffer in the name of detection!

She drove to the Four Pools Estate. How quickly Evesham was spreading out. A new McDonald's had been built in about two weeks earlier in the year and a large new pub in about two months. Soon the countryside would be swallowed up. Agatha realized that she was in danger of becoming one of those people she had hitherto despised—the I-know-they've-got-to-live-somewhere,but-why-can't-it-be-somewhere-else? type of person.

Before she got out of the car, she took a comb out of her handbag and wrenched it down through her lacquered hair until she felt she had flattened it a bit.

As she braced herself to walk up a neat garden path, she was engulfed in a sudden wave of depression. Charles's cavalier treatment of her brought back all her fierce longing for James and her mind began to credit him with warmth and affections that he did not have.

She rang the doorbell.

The door was opened. She recognized Mavis immediately, but Mavis did not recognize her.

'I would like you to know, we go to mass every Sunday,' said Mavis crossly, 'and we don't want anything to do with the likes of you!'

The door began to close.

'I'm not a Jehovah,' said Agatha quickly. 'I was a client of Mr John's.'

The door opened again. 'The one that died?'

'Was murdered, yes. May we talk?'

'Yes, come in.' Mavis had an ordinary sort of face without any particular distinguishing features, pale blue eyes and a surprisingly smooth and shining stylish head of hair.

Mavis, as she led the way into a cosy living-room, did not evince any signs of fear or nervousness. 'Sit down, Mrs . . . ?'

'Raisin. Call me Agatha.'

'Right Agatha. I'll get us some tea. I'd just put the kettle on and I'm dying for a cuppa.'

When Mavis left the room, Agatha looked about her. She had somehow expected the mother of a drug addict and pusher would live in squalor. But the living-room was furnished with a three-piece suite in shades of gold and brown. An electric fire with mock coals glowed cheerfully. There were framed family photographs on the walls and a crucifix over the fireplace. Women's magazines and television guides lay on the coffee-table.

After a short time Mavis entered carrying a tray on which was a fat teapot and china mugs decorated with roses and a plate of cakes, bright with pink and white icing.

'Terrible business, that,' said Mavis, pouring tea. 'And to think I knew him!'

'As a client?' Agatha accepted a mug of very dark strong tea.

'Oh, no, he even took me out for dinner once. What's your interest?'

'I suppose I am by way of being an amateur detective,' said Agatha modestly, for she privately thought there was nothing amateur about her efforts at all.

'Oh, I know. You was in the papers once. Your hubby got bumped off. This is exciting. Just like on telly. Wait till I tell my Jim.'

Jim, the monster! Agatha was beginning to feel bewildered.

'Why did he ask you out and you a married woman?'

'Well, look, it all started with a sort of bet I'd had with Selma Figgs next door. She was saying how Mr John was like a film star. "We couldn't get off with one of those, now could we, Mavis," she says to me. So I said, "I bet you a tenner I can." I knew our Mr John was a bit of a ladies' man and he always seemed to be chatting up right frumps, if you ask me.'

Agatha winced.

'So I spun him a line about an unhappy home-life and all that. I'd pinched it out of one of the soaps, the story, like. So he asks me out for dinner. I told Jim and we had ever such a laugh. "Go on," says Jim, "enjoy yourself. Let the silly sod pay for it."'

'And did he come on to you?' asked Agatha.

'Naw. He was ever so polite and I had a rare good meal. Course it was a bit of a strain, what with me having to keep the story going.'

'Did he ask you about money?'

'Wait a bit. I s'pose he did. Asked what Jim did. I said he was in bathroom sales over at Cheltenham and had a fair enough wage, but what with Betty's university education and our Jack needing new bits for his computer every week, I said it was a miracle we made ends meet.'

She took a sip of tea and wrinkled her brow. 'What else? Oh, I know, he said women like me were very clever and I'd no doubt got a bit put by, and well, I laughed at that one and said every penny I got came from Jim. He never asked me out again. Probably guessed I was a liar.'

Knew you hadn't any money, thought Agatha. She said, 'But when you were telling him those stories—I mean, I heard you telling him your Betty was on drugs. Weren't you afraid someone might inform the police?'

Mavis stared at Agatha round-eyed. Then she said slowly, 'I never thought of that. I mean, everyone chatters on about everything at a hairdresser's, don't they? I mean, when you're talking, what with the noise from the driers and all, you never think anyone is listening. I don't think what I've told you can be of much help. Who would want to bump him off in that cruel way? And why?'

Agatha put down her cup and stood up. 'Well, here's my card. If you hear of anything that might be interesting, let me know.'

'Thanks a lot. You haven't had a cake.'

'Not hungry,' said Agatha with a smile.

Mavis walked her to the door. 'Bye, bye,' she said cheerfully. 'Call round again if you're ever this way.'

Now what do I do? thought Agatha. That was a waste of time.

Inside the trim house she had left, Mavis sat down, her hands to her mouth. Then she gave herself a little shake and smiled up at the photograph of herself on the wall, a photograph Agatha had failed to notice. It showed a much younger Mavis, a blonde and leggy Mavis performing as principal boy in a pantomime production of *Puss in Boots*.

'I could have been a real actress,' said Mavis aloud.

*　　　*　　　*

Agatha went home and fed her cats and played with them for a little. Then she checked her phone to see if there were any messages. None. This was silly. Why not just phone Charles? He could be ill.

She was just about to pick up the phone when it rang. Charles, at last. She picked up the receiver. 'Roy here.' Roy Silver.

'What d'you want?' demanded Agatha sharply.

'I've got a few days off. Thought I might pop down and see you.'

'I'm afraid I'm busy.'

'Oh.'

That 'oh' sounded disappointed, but Agatha calculated sourly that this sudden desire to see her meant that Roy's boss had some public relations scheme he wanted to involve her in.

'And I've got something on the stove,' lied Agatha. 'Look, I'll call you back. Are you at home?'

'Yes, but don't trouble, sweetie,' said Roy huffily.

'I'll ring you.' Agatha put the phone down and dialled Charles's number. The phone was answered by his aunt.

'Oh, Mrs Raisin,' she fluted when Agatha had identified herself. 'Charles is busy with

178

our guests. Is it terribly important?'

'I have found out something that might interest him.'

'Wait a moment and I'll see if he can come to the phone.'

The phone was in the draughty, cavernous wood-panelled hall of Charles's home. Agatha could hear the aunt's heels clopping across the parquet, then the door of the drawing-room opened, a burst of noise and laughter, door closed, silence again.

Charles took so long to answer the phone that Agatha almost hung up. But then she heard the door of the drawing-room open again, that burst of noise and laughter, and then Charles's voice: 'Hello, Aggie.'

'I thought you might have phoned,' said Agatha crossly.

'Oh, you mean our case?'

No, I don't mean our case, Agatha wanted to howl. Don't you remember making love to me?

'Yes, I'll tell you what I've found out.'

Charles listened and then said, 'Seems you do better on your own.'

'Why I phoned,' Agatha pressed on, 'is I wondered when we're going to take that trip to Portsmouth?'

'Can't.'

'Why? Do you think it's a waste of time?'

'No, not that. The most wonderful thing has happened. There's this girl here. Fantastic.

I'm in love.'

'In that case,' said Agatha evenly, 'I won't keep you.'

She hung up and sat down on a chair beside the phone and stared miserably into space.

The silence of the cottage suddenly seemed oppressive. And she was alone. And out there was the maniac who had killed Mrs Darry so brutally. No one wanted Agatha Raisin, except perhaps some murderer who wanted to silence her. There had been a murder committed in Carsely, home of that famous detective, Agatha Raisin, and yet not a reporter had called. But then the police had claimed the credit before. Still, Agatha Raisin had found the body. They probably hadn't told the press that.

She slowly dialled Roy's number. 'I'm sorry I was so rude,' she said when he answered. 'You are most welcome if you want to come.'

'I'll be on the train that gets in around eleven-thirty in the morning.'

'Is that Great Western or Thames Turbo?'

'Don't ask me, sweetie. I was born in the days of British Rail. Why?'

'It's just the trains sometimes get cancelled. If you get stuck, take the train to Oxford and I'll pick you up there.'

'Righto. See you.'

Agatha put down the phone, suddenly grateful for Roy and his thick skin. And if he had a few days free, then perhaps he might

180

like to go to Portsmouth with her. She marvelled at the insensitivity of Charles. How on earth could you bed one woman and then tell her soon afterwards that you were in love with another?

She remembered when she was a little girl going out to play with a gang of boys who had turned nasty and thrown stones at her. She had run home to her mother, blood streaming down her face. 'I told you not to play with the wrong children,' her mother had raged. 'Now, see what happens?'

And I've never learned my lesson, thought Agatha sadly. I've been playing with the wrong children all my life.

*   *   *

It was a blustery day with red leaves swirling down into the station car park when Roy's train cruised in, miraculously on time. Great fluffy clouds sailed across a pale blue sky.

Roy kissed the air on either side of Agatha's face, making *mwaa*, *mwaa* sounds.

'Lovely to see you, Aggie.' Agatha experienced a pang. Charles also called her Aggie.

'You're looking well,' lied Agatha, privately thinking that Roy looked as seedy and unhealthy as ever with his lank hair, white, pinched face, too-tight jeans and bomber jacket.

181

'I'll be healthier after a bit of country air. Tell me how you're getting on with the hairdresser murder.'

As she drove him back to Carsely, Agatha outlined everything she had discovered, but left Charles's name out of it. She ended up by saying, 'Don't feel like a trip to Portsmouth, do you? I feel if I dug into his past I might find something.'

'Give me a day to relax and then maybe we'll go for it.'

'How's business?'

'Business is very good. In fact, I've got another rise. There's a new restaurant in Stratford called the Gold Duck. I took the liberty of booking us a table for dinner.'

At Agatha's cottage, Roy took his bag up to the spare room and then joined Agatha in the kitchen.

'So how's James?'

'I haven't heard. He's abroad somewhere.'

'No reason to let yourself go to seed.'

'What are you talking about?'

'Grey hairs coming through.'

Agatha gave a squawk of alarm and ran up to the bathroom. She peered at the roots of her hair. Her hair grew quickly. Her old colour was beginning to show, along with unmistakably grey hairs.

She ran downstairs again. 'I can't bear it. I've got to get my hair done again. God, I'm spending all my days at the hairdresser's!

Now, who did Garry say everyone was going to? Thomas Oliver, that's it. You'll need to amuse yourself, Roy.'

She phoned and was told there had been a cancellation and they could take her in half an hour's time.

'See you,' she gabbled at Roy and ran out to her car.

The hairdresser's seemed a slicker establishment than either Eve's or Mr John's. There was a friendly atmosphere. She was told to take a seat and that Marie, the owner, would be with her soon. Agatha looked about her curiously. It was very busy, a good sign.

Then Marie Steele joined her. She was an attractive blonde with a friendly smile. 'I've brought a chart of colours,' she said, opening it on Agatha's lap. 'Do you want your hair the same shade?'

'Yes,' said Agatha. 'I'd like it to look as natural as possible.'

'Perhaps this? Or maybe you'd like a little warm touch of auburn?'

Agatha thought of Charles, of James, of lost love. 'Wouldn't it look too false?' she asked cautiously.

'You'll look great. I'll tell Lucy which colour to mix and then I'll blow-dry your hair myself.'

Lucy, a slim, elegant girl who looked like a model, soon arranged Agatha in a chair in the back salon and deftly began to tint her roots. Agatha felt soothed for the first time in days.

The gossip of the hairdresser's surrounded her. Mort, who, it transpired, was Iranian by birth, was chattering non-stop. Gus, a Sicilian, was making his customer laugh; Kevin, a beautiful young man, was washing hair and bringing coffee; and the efficient Marie was here, there and everywhere.

At last Agatha had her hair shampooed and was led through to Marie.

'Now, how do you like it?' asked Marie, raising the hair-drier.

'Sort of smooth. I wear it in a smooth bob.'

'Right. You'll find that tinge of auburn works great.'

She worked busily. The hairdresser's was thinning out. Apart from Agatha, there was only one other customer left.

Finally Agatha looked with delight at her gleaming hair. 'Oh, that's very good,' she said with relief.

'Your hair's in very good condition,' said Marie, sitting down beside her. 'Are you from Evesham?'

'No, Carsely.'

'Raisin! That's it! I knew I'd heard that name. Oh, dear, your husband was murdered.'

'Yes, but I'm over that now.'

'And you were there when John Shawpart died?'

'It was awful.'

'It must have been.'

'You don't expect murder and mayhem at a

hairdresser's,' said Agatha.

Marie laughed. 'I don't know about that. There's times I could have committed murder myself.'

'Awkward customers?'

'No, other hairdressers. It's a bit like the theatre. Lots of rivalries and jealousies. I had most of my staff poached by a rival last year, and just before Christmas. I was so down, I didn't feel like going on. But I've got a great team now.'

'I see that,' said Agatha. 'I'll make another appointment.'

She paid and left, scurrying to the sanctuary of her car in case the wind messed any of the glory of her auburn hair.

*   *   *

'That's better,' said Roy when she arrived home. 'I put your cats in the garden. Have you fed them?'

'Yes. Any phone calls?'

'That aristo friend of yours.'

'Charles?'

'Yes, him.'

'What did he want?'

'Didn't say. Why not call him?'

'Later,' mumbled Agatha.

'So, do we go detecting?'

'Maybe, if you're fit, I'll drive to Portsmouth tomorrow. I spent so long at the hairdresser's, there's not much of the day left. I'll have a bath and change, have a drink and watch some television and then we'll be off. What time did you book the table for?'

'Eight o'clock.'

Agatha forced herself to make up and dress with care, just as if she were about to go out with a glamorous man and not Roy, whom she had first employed as an office boy all those years ago. He was a good public relations officer, particularly with pop groups, who hailed him as one of their own kind.

When she went downstairs, Roy was lounging in front of the television set. 'Aren't you going to change?' demanded Agatha.

'Nobody dresses up to go out for dinner these days,' said Roy, flicking aimlessly through the channels with the remote control.

'I do. So you do. Hop to it!'

Grumbling, Roy went upstairs to change.

*   *   *

The restaurant in Stratford-upon-Avon was crowded. They were given a corner table which commanded a good view of the rest of the customers.

And then Agatha saw Charles. He was sitting with a blonde who had one of those rich-monkey-Chelsea faces. He was telling jokes and laughing uproariously. Agatha noticed with a certain sour pleasure that the girl looked bored.

Roy, on an expense account or had Agatha been paying, would have ordered all the most expensive things on the menu, but as it was, he said he wasn't feeling very hungry and would skip a starter and watched moodily as Agatha ate her way through quail and salad before going on to Steak Béarnaise while he himself had pasta as a main course. He ordered the house wine, saying with a false laugh, 'I don't see any point in ordering anything else. I find the house wine is usually just as good.'

Oh, James, thought Agatha, you were never mean. I feel at this moment, if you walked in the door of this restaurant, I would forgive you anything.

A young man approached Charles's table and hailed his companion. She introduced the newcomer to Charles and asked Charles something. Charles gave a grumpy nod. A waiter was called, another chair brought and the newcomer joined Charles and his lady. She proceeded to sparkle at the newcomer and give him all her attention while Charles, after a few jocular remarks to which neither paid any attention, relapsed into a moody silence.

'Revenge is mine,' said Agatha.

Roy looked at her, puzzled. 'What?'

'Nothing. Yes, I think we'll go to Portsmouth tomorrow.'

Chapter Seven

Agatha sat uneasily on the passenger side of her car as Roy hurtled down the motorways towards Portsmouth the following day. She had wanted to leave her cats in the cottage for the day, but Roy had pointed out that the murderer might come looking for her and destroy her cats in revenge, so Hodge and Boswell had been put in their cat boxes and taken round to the cleaner, Doris Simpson's, for security.

Agatha realized that all her hurt over Charles had dulled the fact that she might be at risk.

'Portsmouth's a big place,' said Roy, 'and there must be an awful lot of hairdressers.'

'We can only ask around a few places,' said Agatha. 'Oh, rats!'

'Rats what?'

'I forgot to switch on the burglar alarm. I'm always doing that.'

'Want to go back?'

'Not now. We've already gone miles. Just need to hope everything will be safe.'

'You know, I think it will be,' said Roy, 'now that I've had time to think about it.'

'How come?'

'Well, how's our murderer supposed to know you're ferreting around?'

'Easy,' said Agatha. 'I think it's one of the ones who were being blackmailed, or someone like Mrs Friendly's husband or Maggie Henderson's husband. Why did you really come to visit me, Roy?'

'Told you. Had a few days off and wanted to see you.'

'It's just when you've turned up before it's mostly been because your boss wants me to do some freelance work.'

'Why do you always pin the worst motives on people?' said Roy crossly. 'Or is the idea of friendship so foreign to your twisted mind?'

'Sorry,' mumbled Agatha. 'Couldn't help wondering.'

'Well, here comes Portsmouth. Park in the centre?'

'Yes, John would have had somewhere right in the centre.'

After several frustrating waits in traffic jams, Roy managed to find a place in a multi-storey car park near Queen Street.

'Now what?' he asked as they walked out into the morning bustle of shoppers.

'Find a library or post office, find a business phone directory and start off at the nearest hairdressing salon.'

*　　　*　　　*

They hit gold at the first salon, called A Cut Above. The proprietress had known John

Shawpart. Her name was Mary Mulligan. 'He had a place round the back of Queen Street,' she said. 'Called Mr John. He and his wife ran it a few years ago. Then the place caught fire. It was arson. The gossip was that they had done it themselves, but John got the money from the insurance. The business was in his name. After that, Elaine Shawpart set up on her own, but she didn't do very well. He did all right after he'd had the place redone. Then he sold up and disappeared and his wife—they'd got a divorce by this time—she sold up and went off as well.'

'Do you happen to know where he lived?'

'Don't know. Wait a bit. I've got some old phone books in the back. Never throw them away. Might be in one of those.'

They waited while she went to look. Driers hummed and the air was full of the bad-egg smell of perms. Beyond the plate-glass windows, people went to and fro. Perhaps one of them had been blackmailed by John, perhaps one of them followed him to Evesham.

'You're lucky,' said Mary, bustling back. 'Here we are. Shawpart. Blacksmith's End. Number two. Blacksmith's End is one of those private builder's projects out on the west of the town.'

She gave them directions.

'Now we're getting somewhere,' said Roy, retrieving the car.

Blacksmith's End turned out to be a quiet cul-de-sac of stone-built houses, very quiet and suburban with manicured lawns at the front and lace curtains at the windows.

They walked up the neat path of number 2 and rang the doorbell, which emitted Big Ben chimes.

A little woman as neat as the house—neat permed hair, neat little features, trim pencil skirt and tailored blouse—answered the door.

'I never buy from door-to-door salesmen,' she said.

'We're simply asking questions about John Shawpart.'

'But I've told the police everything!'

Agatha felt like the amateur she was. Of course the police would have been checking into his background.

'I was the person who found him when he was dying,' said Agatha.

'Come in. I'm Mrs Laver.'

'Agatha Raisin and Roy Silver,' said Agatha as they followed her into a sparklingly clean living-room: three piece suite in Donegal tweed, glass coffee-table, stereo, television; pot plants everywhere, green and lush.

'It must have been dreadful for you, seeing him dying like that,' said Mrs Laver. 'But really, I don't know anything other than we bought the house from him.'

'Did he live here with his wife?'

'No, I gather he moved here after they split

up.'

Agatha looked around at the plants as if for inspiration. 'Did anyone come calling, looking for him, after you moved in here?'

'A couple of women—not together—at separate times. They seemed quite distressed.'

'Did you get their names?'

'No, when I said he had gone, they asked where to, but he didn't leave a forwarding address.'

'That's odd,' said Roy. 'What did you do with the mail?'

'Just marked it "Not Known at This Address" and gave it back to the postman.'

Agatha noticed a faint flush rising up on Mrs Laver's face and the way her hands twisted together nervously in her lap.

'It must have been a bit of a chore,' said Agatha, 'remembering to return all that mail to the postman. I had that to do when I first moved into my cottage. I got so fed up I forgot to return a couple of letters, and after two months, I regret to say I just threw them on the fire. Did you do that?' she demanded sharply.

'Oh, I wouldn't do that. That's criminal!' cried Mrs Laver. 'But . . .'

'But what?' demanded Agatha eagerly. 'You've still got one, haven't you?'

She flushed again. 'It arrived some time after he'd gone from Portsmouth. My husband was away on business and I had the flu, so I put it in the kitchen drawer and thought I'd give it to the postman when I felt better. But then I forgot about it and I was too ashamed to hand it over after all this time.'

Agatha felt her heart beating hard with excitement. 'If you give it to us,' she said, 'we'll give it to the Worcester police. You don't need to worry. We'll just say it got stuck under the doormat.'

'Oh, you couldn't say that,' said Mrs Laver. 'People would think I didn't clean under the doormat in my own home.'

Agatha looked at her impatiently.

'Then we'll say it came through the letter-box and slipped under a crack in the skirting in the hall.'

'But I don't have cracks in the skirting. This is a very sound house!'

Agatha felt like tearing her hair in frustration.

She forced herself to say gently, 'Then I'll just tell them the truth. You were ill. You put it in the kitchen drawer and only remembered it when we called.'

'I won't get into trouble?'

'Not at all. I am very friendly with the police and have hclped them on many cases.'

'Oh, well, I s'pose . . .'

She got up and went through to the kitchen.

Agatha looked at Roy and rolled her eyes. What if the silly woman changed her mind?

But Mrs Laver came back and handed

Agatha a thick brown envelope. Agatha tried not to snatch it.

She stood up. 'We'll be on our way.'

'Aren't you going to see what's in it?' asked Mrs Laver.

'No, we'll leave that job to the police. Come along, Roy.'

They made their escape. As they were getting into the car, Mrs Laver called after them, 'I'd better take a note of your name and address. You're Mrs Anderson, didn't you say?'

'Drive off!' hissed Agatha to Roy. 'Let the silly woman think I'm Mrs Anderson in case she calls the police.'

Roy accelerated off.

'Now when we're clear of this place, stop somewhere,' ordered Agatha, 'and let's have a look at what we've got.'

Roy drove for several streets and then pulled into the side of the road.

Agatha took out the envelope, which she had stuffed in her handbag. She was about to open it when Roy grabbed her hand.

'I don't like this,' he said. 'You'll get us into trouble. This is police evidence.'

'I found it, they didn't,' growled Agatha. 'Get off, Roy. I'll take the responsibility.'

She opened the envelope. It was crammed with fifty-pound notes. 'Must be blackmail money,' she said. 'There's a letter.'

She pulled out one sheet of paper and

opened it. She read, 'This is all I can afford. I think you're a wicked, evil man. After all we were to each other, I can't believe you would do this to me. Harriet.' Agatha counted out the money. 'There's five thousand pounds here!'

'Is there an address?' asked Roy.

'Yes, 14A, Hanson Street, Portsmouth.'

'I'd better stop at a stationer's and get a street map.'

When they had found a map, Hanson Street turned out to be a small street running off London Road in the centre of the town.

'Back to that car park,' grumbled Roy, 'and let's hope there's a space left.'

They had to wait a frustrating half an hour for a car to drive out and leave them a space. They walked to Hanson Street. Fourteen A turned out to be the basement of a shop.

'Doesn't look very prosperous,' said Agatha as they walked down the steps.

Roy rang the bell. A tired-looking middle-aged woman answered the door.

'Harriet?' asked Agatha.

'Yes, who are you?'

'We've brought you this.' Agatha handed her the envelope full of money.

Harriet turned a muddy colour.

'Are you the police?'

'No,' said Agatha. 'Just a couple of people trying to make sure that blackmailing bastard doesn't continue to ruin people from beyond the grave. Can we come in?'

Clutching the envelope tightly, Harriet led them into a large room strewn with coloured fabrics and dominated by a sewing machine.

'You're a dressmaker?' asked Roy.

'Yes, it's a living,' said Harriet wearily. She seemed drained of energy.

She sat down and said, 'You can't blackmail me as well. It was all for nothing.'

'We've only come to help you,' said Agatha. 'We should have given that money and letter to the police. But we didn't.'

'Thank you. I could do with the money.'

'Let's introduce ourselves,' said Agatha briskly. 'I'm Agatha Raisin and this is Roy Silver. I found John Shawpart's body and decided to find out what I could. You don't want us to tell the police about you and I don't want you to tell the police about me. I'll tell you what happened.'

So Agatha told her all about Evesham, about the house being burnt down, about the other women who had been blackmailed.

'Why didn't I even guess he was so evil?' sighed Harriet. 'Move some of those fabrics and sit down. I'm Harriet Worth.'

'So how did he get his claws into you?' asked Agatha.

'In pretty much the same way as he got hold of those other women,' said Harriet. 'I went to the salon to get my hair done. Unlike those other women, my marriage was happy. Luke's got a good job with a computer company. Mr John asked me out and of course I refused. But he laughed it off and he was a wizard at doing my hair and Luke liked my new appearance so I kept going.

'Then John started to look at me in a sort of pitying way and I asked him sharply what was up. At first he said, nothing, but I insisted. He said with a great show of reluctance—he knew what Luke looked like because Luke had called in for me a couple of times at the salon—that he had been out the evening before at a restaurant and had seen Luke with a young blonde. He then made me promise not to tell Luke anything and I did. But I began to get suspicious. It was coming up to Christmas and Luke was often late at the office. He said they were all working flat-out on a new game.'

Harriet heaved a deep sigh. A truck rumbled past on the road above their heads and a child ran a stick along the railings at the top of the steps.

Harriet went on. 'I called up at the office one evening. I never usually went there; in fact, come to think of it, I had only been there once before whcn I forgot my keys. Luke had a new secretary, a pretty young blonde. When I walked in, they had their heads close together and were laughing about something.

'After that, I waited outside the office one evening. I saw them come out together and followed them. Luke and his secretary went into a pub.

'I was devastated. When he at last came home, I asked him why he was so late and he said as usual, pressure of work. I told him I had seen him go to the pub with his secretary and he told me with a sheepish laugh that they had both been working so hard, they had just dropped in for a drink before they both went home.

'I must have gone a bit mad with jealousy because I agreed to go out with John. We had an awful lot to drink. John said, "You can't go home in that state; the salon's just round the corner, I'll make us some coffee." But once in the salon, he took me through to the back and began to take off my clothes and I was so drunk, it all seemed to be happening in a dream. I let him make love to me and then I passed out.'

There was a long silence. Agatha and Roy sat amongst the bright swathes of fabric and waited, although both knew in their hearts what was coming. How could I even have let that bastard touch me, raged Agatha inwardly.

'I told my husband I had gone out with my friend, Julie, to a hen party and had drunk a bit too much and stayed at her place. Then a week later—I'd stopped going to John to get my hair done—he phoned me. He said we had better meet. There was something threatening about his voice. I met him at the salon after

198

hours. He had taken photos of both of us naked—awful photos. He must have set up the camera after I passed out. He said if I paid him five thousand pounds, he would let me have the negatives.'

'Did you have any money?' asked Agatha.

'I had just a little over that in my bank account. Of course I paid, but he didn't let me have the negatives. I was nearly ill with fright. He said coldly he needed more money. One more payment would do it. So I sent that money, the money you brought back to me. I took out a personal loan.'

Agatha looked around. 'Is your husband at work?'

Tears welled up in Harriet's eyes. 'That's the bloody tragedy. After I'd paid that last instalment, Luke left me—for that secretary. The house was in his name. Oh, I suppose I could have got a lawyer. But I was so crushed I just let it all happen.'

'You know Shawpart was murdered?' asked Roy.

'Yes, and when I read it in the papers, I thought if I ever met the woman who did it, I would shake her hand.'

'Might have bccn a man,' suggested Agatha.

'I'm sure it was a woman.'

'What about his wife?'

'They split up just after I started going to Mr John.'

'What was she like?' asked Agatha.

'Well, she wasn't a very good hairdresser, although she didn't know it. She thought she could start up on her own, but her own business soon failed.'

'What did she look like?' asked Roy.

'Blonde, lots of hair, sort of statuesque.'

'Do you think she was in on this blackmailing racket?' asked Agatha.

'I don't know. He only started on me after the divorce.' Harriet clasped her hands and looked at Agatha beseechingly. 'I keep having nightmares about those negatives.'

'I think they were burnt in the fire,' said Agatha soothingly. 'If they hadn't been, the police would have been on to you.'

'Someone's coming,' said Roy as the figure of a man descending the area steps could be seen through the window above.

'I'm not expecting a customer,' said Harriet. She rose and went to the door just as a sharp knock sounded on the outside.

'Luke,' exclaimed Harriet, falling back a step.

Agatha moved like lightning. She picked up the envelope full of money and thrust it into Harriet's open handbag and clicked the clasp shut. She picked up a swathe of material and draped it around her. 'What do you think?' she was asking Roy as Luke walked into the room.

Agatha had imagined that someone called

Luke—a romance name, a cowboy name—
would be a brooding sort of man with
saturnine good looks, not this tubby little
bespectacled man who stood blinking at them
in the gloom of the basement.

In a trembling voice, Harriet introduced
Agatha and Roy.

'I see you're busy,' said Agatha. 'I think this
red would be nice.'

'Too ageing,' said Roy and Agatha threw
him a filthy look.

'We'll be on our way,' said Agatha briskly.
'I've left that payment in your handbag.'

*　　　*　　　*

'So what d'you think?' she asked Roy outside.

'Reconciliation?'

'Poor woman. I hope so. What do we do
now?'

'I'm tired of Portsmouth and we haven't
eaten. I suggest we drive home and stop off on
the road and eat some lovely, greasy,
cholesterol-laden food.'

'But we haven't really got anywhere,' said
Agatha, exasperated.

'Don't know what else we can do. John's
dead, we don't know where the wife is. But
the police will know and they've probably
interviewed her. I've a feeling we're at a dead
end, Aggie.'

Agatha was suddenly engulfed by a wave of

weariness. Was she really interested in this case? Or was she always searching for something to take her mind off James—and now the humiliation of Charles?

Finally comforted by a large, greasy plate of sausages and chips, she slept fitfully on the drive home.

'Hope you haven't had a visit from the murderer,' said Roy cheerfully as they drove up to Agatha's cottage.

'I wish I'd left the burglar alarm on,' grumbled Agatha.

'I was only joking,' said Roy, suddenly nervous.

'We'll go in and check and then go round to Doris Simpson and collect the cats.'

'You first.'

'Coward.'

Agatha walked up the path and then stopped short. Roy collided into her.

'What's up?' he hissed.

'There's a light on in the living-room.'

'Then we go and get a copper. Did you leave a light on?'

'No, honestly. Let's get Fred Griggs.'

Following Agatha's directions, Roy drove to the village police station. It was in darkness, but there was a light on in the flat above. Agatha rang the bell and waited while Fred Griggs lumbered down the stairs.

'Fred,' said Agatha when he answered the door. 'There's a light on in the living-room of my cottage. Someone must be in there.'

'Sure you didn't leave it on?'

'No, Fred. What if it's this murderer waiting for me to come home?'

'I'll just pop on my uniform. Wait here.'

Roy and Agatha waited for what seemed like an age until Fred reappeared.

'Haven't you got a weapon?' hissed Agatha.

'Just my fists. Not even CS gas,' said Fred comfortably.

They drove him back to Agatha's cottage. 'Look at that!' exclaimed Agatha. 'The light's gone out.'

'Maybe you imagined it,' said Fred.

'No, I didn't, did I, Roy?'

'Well, you did say you'd seen it, but maybe we imagined it,' said Roy.

'Can't wait here all night.' Fred walked up to the door. 'Your keys, Mrs Raisin.'

Agatha handed him her door keys. Fred opened the door and Roy and Agatha crowded in behind him.

'Which way's the living-room?'

'Here.' Agatha pointed to the living-room door. Fred opened it and switched on the light.

'Look!' hissed Agatha.

A half-finished glass of whisky stood on a table and a newspaper was dropped on the floor.

'Not yours?' whispered Fred.

Agatha shook her head.

203

'Wait here.' Fred went off and looked in the dining-room and kitchen.

He came back. 'I'll just be taking a look upstairs.'

'I'm coming with you,' Agatha whispered back, not wanting to be left in the hall with only the weedy Roy for protection.

They followed Fred as he crept up the stairs. He opened Agatha's bedroom door. Nothing and no one. Then the bathroom door. Sodden towels lay on the floor.

'I didn't leave it like that,' muttered Agatha.

'Last room,' whispered Fred and opened the door of the spare bedroom. He fumbled and switched on the light.

Sir Charles Fraith lay in bed, fast asleep.

'Seen 'im before with you, Mrs Raisin,' Fred remarked.

'Oh,' said Agatha, weak at the knees with relief. 'It's only Charles. Just leave him.'

They backed out and went downstairs. 'How did your boyfriend get in?' asked Fred with a grin.

'He's not my boyfriend. Just a house guest. I gave him the spare set of keys. Look, Fred, it was very good of you. Roy'll run you back.'

'I'll walk. Nice night for it. Got a full house, hey?' Fred winked at Agatha, slapped her on the bottom and went off whistling.

'Bang goes your reputation, sweetie,' said Roy. 'What a klutz you are! What's with the baronet in the bed? You never told me about him. I mean, I didn't know you were *close*.'

'He's just a friend,' protested Agatha. 'He was staying here for a bit and then he left.'

'I've seen him recently.' Roy frowned. 'Aha, he was in that restaurant in Stratford and with some girl and you never said a word.'

'Can we just leave the whole thing? I'm tired.'

'Have it your way. What's the programme for tomorrow?'

'Nothing. I mean, what's the point? We haven't the resources of the police. I'm going to bed.'

'Come into the living-room a minute and let's have a nightcap. We have to talk.'

'I told you, Roy, I'm dropping the case.'

'Dropping the case,' jeered Roy. 'Hark at the great detective. I want to talk about us.'

Agatha's bearlike eyes narrowed. 'If you've come down here again in the name of friendship to twist my arm into going back into public relations, forget it.'

'I did come down here just to see you, but Mr Wilson did happen to mention . . .' Mr Wilson was Roy's boss.

'I thought so,' said Agatha bitterly. 'You'll need to share a bed with Charles and I hope you'll be very happy together.'

She made for the door. 'I'm going to get my cats. I'll run you to the station in the morning. Early train.'

'But, Aggie . . .'
'Goodnight.'

*   *   *

After Agatha had seen a still-protesting Roy off on the early-morning train, she returned to the cottage to find Charles sitting in the kitchen, wrapped in a dressing-gown and buttering toast.

'What the hell do you mean by creeping back here last night?' snapped Agatha. 'I thought the murderer had broken in. I summoned the local bobby and he found you fast asleep.'

'That's funny.'

'It was not funny at all. So when you've finished your breakfast, please leave.'

Charles looked mildly at the flushed and angry Agatha.

'What's got your knickers in a twist?'

'You, you insensitive, self-absorbed little bastard. You have sex with me, bugger off and then tell me you're in love.'

'Was in love. Was.'

'Then you couldn't have been in love in the first place.'

'You're probably right. Do sit down. I've made some coffee. It's as hot as the steam coming out of your ears.'

Agatha's rage subsided She felt suddenly weary. She sat down.

'Did you not think, Charles, that your behaviour towards me was selfish and insensitive?'

'No, Aggie. I thought we had fun. Then I had these guests and there was this girl, eminently suitable.'

'That doesn't sound like love.'

'It sounds like marriage. I really think I ought to get married. Get an heir and all that.' He waved a piece of buttered toast in the air. 'But she didn't even like me. Met some friend in a restaurant in Stratford and went off with him and left me flat. So I thought, I'd best get back and see what Aggie's up to.'

'Just don't come on to me again!'

'You, Aggie, were the one who crept into my bed.'

'For comfort, not sex.'

'I thought the sex very comfortable.'

'You're not only immoral, Charles, you're amoral.'

'Perhaps. How's the case?'

Agatha sighed. 'Dead in the water. I went to Portsmouth.'

'And?'

Agatha told him about Harriet.

'It's a wonder you didn't stay on in Portsmouth. It's probably crawling with blackmail victims of the wicked hairdresser.'

'John's ex-wife probably knows all about it, but she could be anywhere in the country now. The police have the resources to trace her. I

207

don't. Oh, and I found out something else.'
She told him about Jessie and Mavis.

Charles listened intently. Then he said,
'Run that bit about Mavis past me again.'

Agatha looked at him in surprise but
repeated what had happened during her
interview with Mavis.

'And you believed her?' Charles reached
across the table and fished a cigarette out of
Agatha's packet.

'Why not? She seemed a straightforward,
honest woman. Her home was clean and tidy.
It had the atmosphere of a happy family
home.'

'I'd like to meet her.'

'Why?'

'She just sounds too good to be true.'

'Oh, well, I suppose you won't be satisfied
until you've met her. I never checked to see if
you'd packed and taken your clothes away.'

'No, I rushed off and left them. I'll go and
dress and we'll be off.'

*   *   *

'I wonder if she'll be at home,' said Agatha as
she turned off the by-pass and into the Four
Pools Estate. 'Perhaps we should have phoned
first.'

'Better to surprise her,' said Charles. 'Got
another cigarette?'

'We're nearly there and if you're going to

take up smoking in earnest, then I suggest you buy your own.'

'Filthy habit. There's this hypnotist in Gloucester, said to work wonders.'

'I might try that,' said Agatha. 'I heard about him. But if I do give up smoking, I hope to God I don't turn into one of those morons who goes around making smokers' lives hell. Here we are. You see, you didn't have time for another cigarette.'

As they walked up the path, a curtain twitched. The door opened before they could even ring the bell and Mavis stood there, smiling a welcome.

'How nice to see you again!' she cried. 'Come in. This your husband?'

I like this woman, thought Agatha. It was flattering to be considered Charles's wife, as Charles was much younger than she.

Agatha introduced Charles and they both followed Mavis inside. Mavis bustled off to make tea while Charles walked around the room, peering at photographs. 'Now here's a thing, Aggie,' he whispered. 'Our Mavis was on the stage in her youth.'

'So?'

'So her acting abilities might have fooled you.'

'I'm a good judge of character,' said Agatha huffily.

'Except when it comes to men.'

Agatha was glaring at him as Mavis tripped

209

in bearing the tea-tray.

After she had served tea, Mavis asked brightly, 'So what brings you back?'

Agatha looked helplessly at Charles, who smiled at Mavis and said, 'Aggie here told me what you had said and I wondered why you had lied to her.'

Mavis goggled at him and Agatha stared at Charles in surprise.

Then Mavis's face cleared and she laughed. 'Oh, all that stuff about my Betty being a drug addict.'

'No,' said Charles. 'I believe that was a lie. But I happen to know that Shawpart was blackmailing you.'

There was a shocked silence. 'Mam!' called a child shrilly out on the street. A car drove past, a gust of wind rattled the leaves of the wisteria outside the window and then the room was quiet again.

At last Mavis said in a thin voice, 'So that letter wasn't burnt in the fire.'

Agatha looked to Charles for help, but he was studying Mavis, waiting for her to go on.

'If my husband finds out,' said Mavis, 'it'll be the end of our marriage.'

'He won't,' said Agatha fiercely. 'Tell her, Charles!'

But Charles waited patiently.

'It was like this,' said Mavis. 'He flattered me. He said I should never have left the stage. Oh, he worked on me. He got me when I was feeling down and bored and he supplied a bit of excitement. At first it was just sneaky little coffee meetings and then he said we couldn't talk freely when we were frightened that someone would see us. He invited me to his house. We drank a lot of champagne and he told me . . . he told me he loved me. He was so passionate, he seemed so sincere. And I thought I was the actor! So I went to bed with him. I was so infatuated, I was prepared to run away with him.'

She began to cry. They waited until she had blown her nose and composed herself.

'Then he did not get in touch with you,' prompted Agatha.

'Yes, and I was desperate. I thought I had done or said something. I wrote to him. When he phoned and said he wanted to meet me, I was over the moon. Then he told me unless I paid him he would send the letter to my husband.'

'I thought you didn't have any money of your own,' said Agatha.

'I lied. I had a bit put by. But then what seemed like a miracle happened. He was murdered. No, it wasn't me, although I dreamed of it. Don't go to the police.'

'We won't go to the police,' said Agatha. 'And there's no evidence. All the evidence was burnt in the fire.'

Mavis's eyes narrowed. 'So where the hell do you two get off, tormenting me?' She stood up. 'Get out of here!'

'We're only trying to find out who did it,' said Agatha patiently.

'That's a job for the police. I've a good mind to report you.'

'If you do that,' said Charles, 'we'll be obliged to tell the police what we know about you.'

Mavis crumpled. 'I'm sorry. But it has all been so horrible. I'm sorry I got angry.'

'That's all right. We'll be off,' said Charles. 'Think no more about it.' He stood aside to let Agatha past, and then whipped round.

'You weren't ever married to John Shawpart, were you?'

'No!'

'Know anything about his wife?'

'He said something about her being jealous of him. She was a hairdresser as well.'

They thanked her and left.

'How did you know about her, Charles?' asked Agatha as they drove off.

'I didn't. I just guessed.'

'Why? How?'

'Well, Shawpart seems to have been a cunning bastard. If there was no money in it, he dropped them.'

'So what made you think he hadn't dropped Mavis? She told me she had told him that she hadn't any money and I believed her.'

'It was a lucky guess. I thought it was worth a try. I mean, she did tell him all those lies

212

about herself to get his interest. She must have told him the one about her drug-dealing daughter was a lie or he wouldn't even have bothered bedding her. He'd just have used that.'

'Let's go back and make some notes,' said Agatha. 'Interested again?'

'Sort of. There might be something I've missed.'

*   *   *

'Now,' said Charles, sitting over a sheet of paper at Agatha's kitchen table half an hour later, 'let's see what we've got. We've got Mavis Burke. She could have put ricin in his vitamin pills. Then there's the receptionist, Josie. She was in love with him. Mr and Mrs Friendly. Maggie Henderson or *her* brutal husband. Harriet of Portsmouth or her husband.'

'But Harriet's husband left her for the secretary.'

'So *she* said. Could be another liar. She could have looked shocked when Luke turned up on her doorstep, not at seeing him again but in case you guessed she'd been telling a pack of lies. Anyone else?'

'Jessie Lang, but that's a non-starter.'

Charles leaned back in his chair. 'Yes, let's think about Jessie Lang. Why would our philandering blackmailer waste his time on a bit of crumpet with no money? Not his scene.'

'I'm sure she was telling me the truth,' said Agatha hotly. 'You think she's lying because I got a lot more out of her than you did!'

'It's a thought all the same. Then there's Mrs Shawpart.'

'But we don't know where she is!'

'Don't we? We don't know how long any of the married women suspects have been married. Could be Mavis.'

'Who miraculously produces a teen-aged daughter and son after about a year?'

'Did you see any photos of her children? I didn't. I don't trust Mavis one bit.'

'We're forgetting Mrs Darry,' said Agatha. 'Poor Mrs Darry. What on earth could she have possibly found out that we didn't?'

'That's a point. Why don't we trot along to the vicarage and ask Mrs Bloxby for some gossip?'

*　　　*　　　*

As they approached the vicarage door, Agatha found herself hoping the vicar was not at home to start shouting in front of Charles about 'that dreadful woman'.

But Mrs Bloxby answered the door with her usual glad smile of welcome. Agatha knew her to be a busy woman and yet she never appeared to be flustered by the unheralded arrival of visitors.

214

'This is nice,' said Mrs Bloxby. 'Come into the kitchen. I've got some fresh coffee ready.'

Agatha sat down at the kitchen table and half-closed her eyes, letting the peace of the vicarage wash over her. Why did she always create such an insane world for herself, she wondered, where the totally unacceptable became the acceptable? What was she doing sitting here companionably with Charles? She should have told him to get lost, she should have said she would never see him again. And, what was even more important, she should stop this silly business of pretending to be a detective and let the police get on with it.

Mrs Bloxby put down thin china mugs of coffee in front of them and a plate of chocolate biscuits before sitting down herself. 'You were away yesterday, Agatha?'

'Yes.'

'The press were suddenly all over the place. You know, there were only a few directly after the murder. The police must have released that there was some connection between Mrs Darry and the murder of the hairdresser, although they appear to have released nothing about John Shawpart's blackmailing activities. You see, there wasn't much of a fuss before because the press thought it was just another murder of a pensioner in the Midlands. How awful that sounds! Just another murder. But there are so many. The longer people live, the more pensioners there are, and the more that get murdered. They're such an easy, vulnerable target.'

'Someone will be after Aggie next,' said Charles.

'I'm not a pensioner,' snapped Agatha.

'So were you investigating yesterday?' asked Mrs Bloxby.

'Went to Portsmouth.'

'With her toy boy,' murmured Charles.

'Now why does that ring a bell? Portsmouth,' mused Mrs Bloxby, ignoring Charles.

'That's where John Shawpart came from,' said Agatha.

'So it is. But there's something else. . . . Never mind, it'll come to me. So how did you get on?'

Agatha told her about Harriet. 'That poor woman!' exclaimed Mrs Bloxby.

'If she was telling the truth,' Charles put in. 'Aggie here is very gullible.'

'I think that remark was uncalled for,' said Mrs Bloxby.

'Tell him about Mavis,' said Agatha.

Mrs Bloxby listened intently and then said, 'But it does not follow that Harriet was lying. Why should she lie? She paid, didn't she, and it's thanks to Agatha that she got that five thousand pounds back.'

'There're too many suspects,' said Agatha gloomily. 'Because of Mavis, I think everyone has been lying to me. When I overheard that woman telling John she would kill him, he said it was the woman in the shop next door talking to her husband, but she said she wasn't married. So she wasn't married, but what if John had got his clutches into *her*?'

'So where do you go from here?' asked Mrs Bloxby.

'I don't know,' said Agatha wearily.

Charles nibbled on a chocolate biscuit. Then he said, 'What about us visiting Bill Wong? He surely knows something about that wife of John's. In fact, he probably knows a hell of a lot more than we do.'

Agatha brightened. 'That's an idea. Let's go and see Bill. In fact, I think we'll do that now. Thanks for the coffee.'

She and Charles got up.

Agatha turned in the doorway. 'I quite forgot to ask you. Do you know where Mrs Darry came from? Where did she live before she came to Carsely?'

'How stupid of me,' exclaimed Mrs Bloxby. 'How could I have forgotten?'

'Forgotten what?'

'Why, Portsmouth, of course. Mrs Darry came from Portsmouth!'

Chapter Eight

'Phew!' said Agatha. 'I'm feeling as if I've just been struck by a blinding flash of the obvious.'

'What do you mean?' asked Charles as they walked back to the cottage.

'Why, Mrs Darry, of course. She wouldn't have been clever enough to ferret out anything dangerous about the murderer in such a short time. She must have known Mr John in Portsmouth! So it follows she probably knew who murdered him.'

'How could she know that?' asked Charles. 'She'd just have been in the same fix as we are. All those people being blackmailed. Who to choose from?'

'Stands to reason it must have been someone from Portsmouth.'

'Harriet?'

'I'm sure it's not Harriet. Damn. Let's go in and have some coffee and think before we see Bill Wong.'

When they were seated over the coffee-cups, Agatha said, 'If only we could find the wife.'

'Maybe the police have already found her. They're bound to have found her.'

'You see, perhaps we've become all messed up by this blackmail business. Perhaps it was just marital hate.'

'Trust me,' said Charles. 'When you've got a blackmailer in the picture, then someone is going to murder him.'

'Anyway, I think I'll call on Bill Wong.'

'Shouldn't you phone him first?'

Agatha hesitated. Then she said, 'No, let's just go. Unless you have anything else planned?'

'No,' said Charles gloomily. 'I'm off women.'

Meaning I don't count as a woman, thought Agatha.

* * *

As they drove to Mircester, Agatha admired the autumn colours of the trees. 'How quickly the seasons change now,' she remarked. 'It seems as if someone drew a line between summer and autumn. Not so long ago we were sweltering and then suddenly, autumn fell. Do you think it's the ozone layer?'

'Probably it's disintegrating under all the cigarette smoke from people like you.'

'Nasty. I wonder if that hypnotist in Gloucester is any good.'

'You'll never know until you try.'

'It's the mean people like you who manage to cut down on their smoking, Charles.'

'You're just jealous because you're a confirmed addict. Why don't you just stop now?'

There was a silence and then Agatha said suddenly, 'Why don't I? When we get to Mircester, I'm going to take the cigarettes out of my handbag and throw them in the nearest rubbish bin.'

'And what about that carton you've got at home?'

'We shall burn them ceremoniously on the fire when we get home.'

As soon as the words were out of her mouth, Agatha felt the hunger for a cigarette. She would fight it. It was only a matter of will-power.

They parked outside police headquarters in Mircester. 'Probably be out on a job,' said Charles. 'We should have called.'

'We'll try anyway.'

They were in luck. They were shown into a room and told that Bill would be with them shortly.

He arrived and greeted them with the words, 'I hope you two have been keeping your noses clean.'

'Yes,' said Agatha huffily. 'But we can't help being curious. We just wanted to know if you'd found Shawpart's wife.'

'I don't see that there is any harm in telling you that we haven't. Why?'

'She could be in Evesham.'

'She was last heard of in Glasgow. A friend of hers got a postcard from her.'

'What friend?' asked Agatha eagerly.

'I'm not telling you. When you call on someone, Agatha, the next thing we know, that person has mysteriously died.'

'Mrs Darry was from Portsmouth,' said Agatha eagerly. 'That was the connection.'

'Obviously,' said Bill. 'But we do not know what she found out.'

'Can't you give us any help?' asked Agatha.

'I can't,' said Bill. 'You caused enough trouble by masquerading as Shawpart's sister and then lying about driving past the house. Agatha, please just leave it alone.'

'Well, if you don't want my help . . .'

'I DON'T!'

'There's no need to shout.'

'Look, Agatha, you've nearly got yourself killed before and I don't want to see that happening again.'

But Agatha was deeply offended. 'Come along, Charles,' she said haughtily. 'Bill obviously doesn't want to tell us anything.'

Charles winked at Bill and meekly followed her from the room.

'He's only concerned for you, Aggie,' said Charles mildly when they were outside.

'Tough,' grumbled Agatha. 'He can sit there and rot. I shall never offer him my help again.'

'Bit hard. He's gone out on a limb for you before.'

'Like when?'

'Like when he faxed all that stuff to you in

Cyprus. Let's go back to your cottage and cool down.'

* * *

After a late and silent lunch, Charles suddenly said he would go home and check out things there. Agatha could think of nothing to say or suggest to keep him. She heartily wished there could be some way she could find out more about what the police had discovered.

She pottered around aimlessly for the rest of the day, played with her cats and fed them, watched some television, or rather flicked backwards and forwards through the channels, and then decided to have an early night.

But Agatha tossed and turned. She kept going over what she had found out again and again. Faces swam in front of her—Maggie, Jessie, Harriet, Josie and the rest. At last, she felt her eyes close. She would forget about the whole thing, go to that nice hairdresser, Marie, and get her hair done and maybe buy a new dress.

Suddenly her eyes shot open. She could almost hear Marie's voice talking about the jealousies and rivalries in the hairdressing business. And wait a bit! John Shawpart had said the same thing. And who was it had said that John's wife had been jealous of him?

Her heart beat faster. And who was it who had turned up in Evesham after John's death, set up business and taken over his staff?

Eve!

Mrs Shawpart had been described as blonde and statuesque. But then in these days of clever dying and tinting, Eve could have changed her hair from blonde. It was a long shot, but it was worth a try.

*   *   *

The next day she phoned up Eve's and told Josie she insisted that Eve herself did her hair. Josie sulkily said she could fit her in at three that afternoon, although Agatha was sure that the day was probably full of free appointments.

Agatha felt she should tell someone what she was about to do . . . well, just in case. If she told Bill, he would order her not to go. But if she told Charles, perhaps he could phone the police.

She dialled Charles's number. Fortunately he answered the phone himself. He listened carefully and to her relief did not tell her she was behaving like an idiot.

'Tell you what, Aggie,' said Charles. 'I've got a friend in the village who's a TV sound man. I'll see if I can get him and bring him over. He'll put a mike on you and then we'll wait across the road with the headphones on and if there is even a glimmer that she's the one we want, I'll call the police.'

'Don't be long,' urged Agatha.

She waited impatiently and, as the hands of the clock crept around to two in the afternoon, was beginning to wonder if she should go ahead without them. But suddenly Charles's car drove up, and Charles got out followed by a tall thin man.

'Right, Aggie,' said Charles when she had let them in, 'Brian here will just fix you up and then you can get off.'

Agatha was wearing a trouser suit. The sound pack was clipped on to the waistband of her trousers and the small mike fastened on her collar. 'She might see that little black thing,' said Charles. 'Have you got a brooch or something?'

Agatha went up to her jewel box and found a gaudy piece of costume jewellery. 'That's quite horrible,' commented Charles, 'but it will stop her noticing the microphone.'

They all set off in Charles's car.

'I never thought about this,' exclaimed Agatha suddenly. 'How can I start accusing her of murder in front of her staff?'

'Try anyway,' said Charles. 'Say you want a quiet word with her.'

'Okay, I'll try.'

Agatha was feeling nervous on two counts. First, if Eve were the murderess, then she might be in real danger. And second, if Eve were not, Agatha felt she would make a terrible fool of herself in front of this sound man.

They parked and then walked along the High Street. 'Now,' said Charles, 'we'll wait across the street in this doorway. Go to it, Aggie, and best of luck.'

The day was sunny and pleasantly warm. People came and went in the High Street with their amiable, non-threatening Evesham faces. Agatha suddenly felt silly. In the clear sunshine, her idea began to seem mad. All that would happen would be that she would end up with a truly dreadful hair-style.

Agatha pushed open the door and went in.

Josie was painting her nails and did not look up. 'I've an appointment,' snarled Agatha. 'Jump to it!'

Josie gave a stage sigh and said, 'Follow me,' and, waving her painted nails in the air to dry them, led Agatha through to the wash-basins. Eve was sitting reading a magazine. There were no other customers.

'That's all right, Josie,' said Eve, putting down her magazine. 'You can take the rest of the day off. I'll attend to Mrs Raisin. Would you like a coffee first, Mrs Raisin?'

'No, thank you.' Agatha did not want to risk getting coffee laced with ricin.

Josie went off. Eve unhitched a gown and held it out to Agatha.

'I'd like a word with you first . . . Mrs Shawpart,' said Agatha.

'Who's she?'

'You are the wife of the hairdresser who was murdered, aren't you?' demanded Agatha.

Eve looked at her in bewilderment. 'I never even knew John Shawpart,' she said. 'I had a hairdressing establishment in Worcester and moved here. Whatever gave you such an odd idea?'

'Despite the colour of your hair,' pursued Agatha, although she was beginning to feel stupid and acutely conscious of Brian and Charles listening in, 'you fit the description given me of Mrs Shawpart. Your husband divorced you and collected all the insurance from your salon when it burned down. You were jealous of his success.'

Eve looked at her wearily. 'You are talking absolute rubbish. Wait a minute.'

She went away and came back with a business card. 'That was the business I had last year and I was in business in Worcester for ten years. Ask anyone.'

Agatha dismally looked down at the business card. It said, 'Eve's Hairdressing,' with an address in the Foregate in Worcester.

'I'm sorry,' she mumbled.

'Well, we all make mistakes. Come over to the wash-basin. What on earth gave you such a mad idea?'

Agatha allowed her to put the gown on and then sat down meekly at the wash-basin.

'I'd been investigating because I was the

226

one who found him when he was dying,' she said. 'He was a blackmailer.'

'Never!'

'Yes. So at first I thought that it might be one of the people he had been blackmailing and then I suddenly thought it might be his wife, and since you suddenly appeared and took over his staff, I leaped to the wrong conclusion that you might be his wife. I'm sorry.'

'Don't worry about it. Lean your head back. Comfy?' Agatha nodded.

*   *   *

Across the road, Brian and Charles, with their headphones on, looked at each other. Brian removed his. 'May as well take these things off.'

'Keep listening,' said Charles. 'Poor Aggie. Let's hear just how much of a fool she's making of herself.'

*   *   *

'But I tell you one thing,' said Agatha. 'I plan to go on and on until I track down the missing Mrs Shawpart.'

Eve shampooed Agatha's head with strong fingers. Suddenly those fingers buried themselves in her hair and held her head in a strong grip.

'Did you tell anyone you were coming here?' asked Eve.

'No,' lied Agatha.

'Just as well.'

'Why?'

'Because, you interfering bitch, you're not going to get out of here alive.'

Across the road, Charles whipped out a mobile phone and called the police.

Agatha tried to get up and then yelped in pain as Eve held tightly on to her hair.

'He had it coming to him,' said Eve viciously. 'He always said the success of the salon in Portsmouth was due to his talents. I thought, I'll show the bastard. After the divorce, I set up a rival salon, but he poisoned people's minds against me.'

Agatha forced herself to remain still, hoping against hope that the microphone was working. 'And did you blackmail women as well?'

'I didn't even know about that, not until just before I left Portsmouth, when some stupid woman came whining to me.'

'You set his house on fire? How come you had the keys?'

'I came back and cosied up to him. John was so vain, he thought he was irresistible. We spent a few nights together for old times' sake and I got him to give me a set of keys.'

'But why set his house on fire?' Keep her talking and pray to God Charles has phoned the police, thought Agatha. Her knees were trembling and sweat from her forehead trickled down her face.

'Because I didn't want the police finding our marriage certificate or any papers.'

'But he might have told someone that you were around!'

'He laughed and swore he hadn't. Liked to keep his ladies thinking there was no one else but them in his life.'

Agatha strained her ears for the wail of a police siren but heard only the drivelling Muzak that was playing in the salon.

'But why didn't the police find you? If you've changed your name by deed poll, they'd have got on to it.'

'Got forged papers in Glasgow. You can always get forged papers if you're prepared to pay the price. Set up a bank account in my new name. Easy.'

'And where did you get the ricin?'

'When I was married to John, one of our customers gave me some castor-oil beans he'd got in India. He told me about the poison. I put them away in a drawer and forgot about them, until I realized how I could use them. I got another of my crooked friends in Glasgow to extract the poison and put it in a syringe. I simply injected it into the bastard's vitamin pills and sat back and waited for results.'

'But why?' asked Agatha. 'So he was cheating on you. Why kill him?'

'He did worse than cheat on me,' hissed Eve. 'He said I was no good as a hairdresser. He took away my customers. No one insults my hairdressing skills.'

'You were jealous of him,' said Agatha. 'You bloody hairdressers are a lot of prima donnas. You killed him out of jealousy. But you were lucky. You could have been seen in Evesham. You could—'

Eve banged Agatha's head painfully against the basin. 'Shut up. I'm bored with you, you dreary old frump. He got into your knickers, didn't he?' She banged Agatha's head painfully again and Agatha yelled.

Keep her talking, thought Agatha although her head hurt and she was terrified.

'So you were never in Worcester?'

'No, I got some business cards printed in a machine, just in case.'

'And what about Mrs Darry?'

'The old cow recognized me and—'

All at once Eve stiffened. The salon was suddenly filled with the wail of police sirens.

Eve released Agatha's hair.

Screaming like a banshee, Agatha hurtled out of the chair just as police poured into the shop. She did not wait for all the joy of hearing Eve being cautioned, she went straight out of the shop into Charles's arms.

'What kept them so long?' she kept sobbing over and over again.

At the end of a long day of police questions and statements, Agatha and Charles finally found themselves alone in Agatha's cottage.

'And the only praise I got from Bill,' said Agatha sourly, 'was that he supposed it took one rank amateur to find another.'

'John's wife certainly had the luck of the devil,' said Charles, nursing a brandy. 'Your head's still stiff with shampoo. Aren't you going to wash it off?'

Agatha gave a squawk of alarm. 'You should have said something before this. I wonder how she planned to kill me?'

'Well, she was banging your head. Probably meant to keep on banging it until you looked like Mrs Darry.'

'And then what would she have done?'

'Well, she had one false identity. Probably planned to flee back to Glasgow and get another. I'm starving. Go and wash your hair and I'll take you out for dinner.'

'Right. Don't drink all that brandy.'

Agatha went up to the bathroom and took off her clothes and threw everything she had worn into the laundry basket. Then she switched on the shower and took a bottle of shampoo and stood under the jet and shampooed her hair vigorously.

Then she stepped out and towelled her hair. She threw that towel on the floor and then dried her face. Her head felt strangely cold. She looked in the mirror and then began to scream.

She had not locked the bathroom door. Charles came bounding up the stairs, crashed open the door and then burst out laughing.

Too distressed to bother about her nakedness, Agatha bent down and picked up the towel with which she had dried her hair. Clumps of wet hair fell out of it on to the bathroom floor.

'The bitch must have used a depilatory,' said Charles when he could.

Aware at last that she was stark-naked, Agatha wrapped a bath-towel about herself. 'What on earth am I to do?' she wailed.

'Buy a wig. You're not completely bald. You've got little bits of hair sticking up from your head. Gosh, you do look funny.'

'I'm not going out for dinner looking like this.'

'Nonsense. Just wrap a scarf around your head.'

'Go away, Charles, until I recover.'

Charles went off laughing. Agatha gloomily dried herself and dressed and wrapped a pink chiffon scarf around her head, turban-fashion.

As she went down the stairs, the doorbell rang. 'Masses of press out there,' said Charles cheerfully. 'Want to go out and address them? Your moment of glory has come.'

'No,' said Agatha, shrinking back. 'Not like

this. Charles, I don't want anyone to know what she did to me!'

'Why?'

'It'll make me a laughing-stock. You talk to them. Leave me out of it.'

Charles shrugged and then went outside. Agatha could hear the sound of his light upper-class voice chatting away happily.

At last he came in. 'That should keep them happy,' he said. 'They've promised not to bother us again tonight.'

'Well, at least the police can't take the glory away from me,' said Agatha. 'It'll be in all the papers tomorrow about how I solved the case. What about dinner?'

'If you'll be all right, I think, on second thoughts, I'll take my stuff and go home. The aunt is beginning to fret that I'm neglecting my duties on the estate.'

Agatha was disappointed. 'If you must, you must. I could have done with a bit of company tonight.'

'I'll phone you.' He went upstairs and reappeared a short time later carrying a suitcase.

He gave her a peck on the cheek. 'Don't worry. Your hair'll soon grow in again. I'll phone you.'

And then he was gone.

Agatha sat down and stared about her. The cats jumped on her lap and she stroked them. The doorbell rang sharply, making her jump.

The press. Perhaps she had been silly to leave it all to Charles. She checked in the mirror to make sure the pink scarf was in place and then opened the door.

'Oh.'

Mrs Bloxby stood there. 'I just heard about your catching the murderess. I wanted to make sure you had some company, otherwise I'll stay with you.'

'Would you?' said Agatha, but peering around the vicar's wife to make sure all the press had gone. 'Charles has left.'

'That's a bit cavalier of him, surely?'

'Oh, there's no explaining Charles,' said Agatha wearily. 'Do come in. I am glad to see you.'

Mrs Bloxby put a large bag down on the hall floor. She crouched down and opened it and lifted out a casserole. 'I didn't think you would be in the mood to cook anything, so I brought a rabbit casserole.'

'How kind. Oh, you're looking at my scarf. That hairdresser from hell shampooed my hair with depilatory.'

'Good heavens! How awful! Well, it'll grow in again soon enough.'

'I hope James doesn't reappear until it does.'

Mrs Bloxby picked up the casserole and headed for the kitchen. 'Still James, is it? I was sure you'd got over him.'

'It's not as bad as it was,' said Agatha,

unwinding the scarf from her head and following the vicar's wife into the kitchen. 'Just a sort of dull ache.'

Mrs Bloxby lit the oven and placed the casserole in it. 'Won't be long,' she said, straightening up. 'I've got potatoes and dumplings in it as well. So how did you get on with the press?'

'I didn't want them to see me like this,' said Agatha. 'Do take off your coat and sit down. I'll just open a bottle of wine. Yes, I felt I would be a laughing-stock, so I sent Charles out to speak to them.'

'Was that wise?'

'What do you mean?'

'It was your moment of glory. And with that chiffon scarf wrapped around your head like a turban, it looked all right.'

'I was so upset. I was recovering from the shock. Perhaps I should have spoken to them. I wonder if I can ask you a favour? Can you nip out in the morning and get me all the newspapers?'

'Gladly.'

They had a pleasant dinner. Agatha felt all the horrors receding and was almost tempted at one point to tell the vicar's wife that she would be all right on her own, but the thought that the horror of it all might return as soon as she put her head on the pillow made her decide to let Mrs Bloxby stay.

Agatha, to her amazement, slept heavily and did not awake until nine the following morning.

There was a note on the kitchen table from Mrs Bloxby. 'Sorry I had to dash back to the vicarage. Some local emergency. Hadn't time to get the newspapers. Don't worry about them. I would have a quiet day at home if I were you.'

'But I just have to see the newspapers,' said Agatha aloud, thinking that it must have been some pretty dire emergency to take the vicar's wife away and make her not carry out her promise.

She decided she could not wait. The local post office stores only stocked a few newspapers and if one did not get there early, they were usually all sold out. Wrapping her scarf round her head in a turban, Agatha went out to her car and drove down to Moreton-in-Marsh. She felt very famous. Her picture would be all over the newspapers. They hadn't photographed her last night, but because of the murder of her husband, she knew they all had her photograph on file.

She bought all the newspapers and paid for them, not looking at the headlines, wanting to savour them when she got to her car.

She started with the *Express*. There was nothing on the front page. She flipped through it. Suddenly, there staring up at her was a large photograph of Charles with the headline, 'BARONET SOLVES HAIRDRESSING MURDER.'

She skimmed down the type. She was only mentioned as 'a friend.' But they knew it was she who had solved the murder, for they had all been outside her cottage. She went through newspaper after newspaper with growing fury. Only two of them had actually mentioned her by name. They all said that the clever baronet had sent a woman friend in to lay a trap for Eve and then had alerted the police.

Agatha drove grimly back to her cottage and tried to get Charles on the phone, but his aunt said he had gone off travelling somewhere.

She walked along to the vicarage.

Mrs Bloxby answered the door and gave her a shame-faced look. 'You knew,' Agatha accused her. 'That's why you didn't leave the newspapers for me.'

'Yes,' said Mrs Bloxby on a sigh. 'Come in. I cannot understand why most of them left your name out of it.'

'Charles,' said Agatha bitterly. 'He took all the glory and they had a real-live sleuth baronet prepared to charm them, so they forgot about me. I was the one who solved it. Do you know the motive? Jealousy. Nothing but jealousy. Not because he was unfaithful to her. I never knew before that the world of hairdressing was so riven with hates and jealousies.'

'I suppose it's just like the theatre, and if they're not very good at the job, the bigger the vanity,' said Mrs Bloxby. 'I'll get you a coffee. Come through to the kitchen. Did you find out why she killed Mrs Darry?'

Agatha trailed after her. 'The police told me they found a note from Mrs Darry to Eve, saying, "I know who you are and I am going to the police. If you want to talk about it before I call them . . ." and then gave her address.'

'But why would she do that? Did she want to blackmail Eve?'

'I think Mrs Darry, God rest her soul, was a nasty woman and I don't think she thought for a moment that Eve was a murderess. I think she just wanted to torment her. Well, she paid for it.'

Agatha sighed wearily. She thought of James, she thought of Charles. 'I'm sick of everything. I'm sick of men. All men are rats.'

'No, only the ones you seem to associate with. You are worth better, Mrs Raisin.'

'I don't think I'll ever forgive Charles.'

'I think it was probably the title. It's supposed to be a classless society, but newspapers do get carried away by a title.'

'I think Charles made sure he got all the glory and left none for me. I'm sick of everything. I'm sick of Carsely.'

'Poor old Carsely had nothing to do with

238

you going bald or some baronet upstaging you.'

'True, but I want to kick someone or something.'

'Don't kick me. Have some coffee.'

*   *   *

After Agatha had left, the vicar came into the kitchen. 'Has that dreadful woman gone?'

'I happen to be very fond of her. I think she is very brave.'

'I saw her arriving. She looked stupid with that scarf round her head. Middle-aged women should never wear pink.'

'That awful hairdresser used a depilatory on her. She's quite bald.'

The vicar began to laugh.

'It's not funny,' said Mrs Bloxby sharply.

'So what did she say when you told her the love of her life was due back?'

'James Lacey? No, Alf. I did not. I wish she would get over him. I couldn't tell her. With her looking like that, she would fly into a panic.'

'Should have told her and given the old girl time to buy a wig,' said the vicar heartlessly.

Mrs Bloxby put a mug of coffee down in front of him.

'Really, Alf,' she said, 'there are times when I wonder whether you are a Christian at all!'

239

Epilogue

Two days later, Bill Wong called on Agatha. 'What have you done to your hair?' he asked.

'It's a wig,' said Agatha. 'Eve used depilatory instead of shampoo.'

'Oh my. It's an odd sort of wig, Agatha.' Agatha's face peered out at him from a long page boy of brown nylon hair.

'There's a good hairdresser in Evesham, Marie. Her son, Brian, over at Bidford-on-Avon, is making me up a proper one. I hate this one. I bought it in a store and it feels hot and scratchy. Excuse me a moment, I think I'll take it off and put a silk scarf on instead.'

She went upstairs and returned shortly with a Paisley silk scarf wrapped around her head. 'That's better. Now are you here to lecture me about the folly of interfering in police work?'

'No, I'm here to thank you,' said Bill. 'We were still chasing the blackmailing angle, although we were still looking for the wife. But you did put yourself at great risk. We've got that tape Charles recorded.'

'Charles!' Agatha spat out.

'Yes, tell me about that. How come he got all the headlines?'

Agatha told him.

'You do pick 'em,' said Bill sympathetically.

'Well, I've finished with him.'

'And what about Lacey?'

'I've forgotten about him,' lied Agatha. 'Tell me about Mrs Darry. What happened there? Did Mrs Shawpart say anything in her statement?'

'Oh, yes. She talked and talked. She's a real psychopathic villain. Mrs Darry recognized her and—would you believe it?—Mrs Darry tried to blackmail *her*. So all the dreadful Eve did was to mildly agree to the terms and say she would call on her. But there's worse to come. Mrs Darry made things easy by telling her about the back way, said she didn't want anyone in the village to see her calling.'

'Somehow that makes me feel a bit easier in my mind,' said Agatha slowly. 'I thought she was a completely innocent victim.'

'If Mrs Darry had come to us, she would still be alive. And think of that, Agatha, next time you decide to take matters into your own hands.'

Agatha was almost on the point of confessing to Bill that she had been in Shawpart's house when it was set on fire, but stopped herself. Bill was a friend, but first and foremost he was a police officer.

'So what lies ahead for you now?' asked Bill.

'I don't know,' said Agatha wearily. 'I think I'll get some good books and have a few quiet days.'

'Tell you what, I've a few days owing to me

next week. I'll come and pick you up. Mum and Dad would like to see you.'

Agatha blinked at him, knowing that Mr and Mrs Wong did not like her at all. 'That's very kind of you,' she said. She could think of some excuse later on.

*   *   *

For the next few days, Agatha relaxed, attended a meeting of the Carsely Ladies' Society, read and went for long walks. Marie phoned to say her wig was ready and once she had collected it and put it on, she began to feel very much like her old self.

That was until she was buying some groceries in the village shop when she heard the assistant say, 'I've boxed up Mr Lacey's groceries. When are they to be delivered?'

Agatha froze.

A voice shouted from the back shop. 'Five o'clock this evening. That's when he's arriving.'

Agatha paid for her groceries and fled home. James could not see her in this wig.

She had dreamt of him and thought of him and now that he was nearly back in Carsely again, she suddenly felt she could not face him, could not face returning to all that pain and frustration again, and with a nearly bald head.

She plunged into action. Doris Simpson was

phoned and said yes, she would look after the cats. Agatha packed a suitcase feverishly.

At four o'clock, she got into her car and drove out of Carsely. She had no idea where she was going. All she knew was that she just had to get away.

*   *   *

James Lacey arrived at his cottage. He was about to put his key in the door when he stiffened. For standing outside Agatha's cottage was Sir Charles Fraith, clutching an enormous bouquet of flowers. The two men stared at each other. Charles rang the bell.

Agatha's cleaner, Doris Simpson, who had come to check out the cottage and see that the cats were all right, opened the door.

'Why, Sir Charles,' she said. 'You've missed Agatha by about an hour.'

'Darling!' shouted Charles. 'Aren't you going to ask me in?'

The cleaner looked puzzled but stepped back. Charles sailed in and slammed the door behind him.

James stood for a moment, glaring, then he too went inside and slammed the door.